THE WINGMAN

CATHRYN FOX

people. If you would like to share this book with another person, please purchase an additional copy for each recipient. If you're reading this book and did not purchase it, or it was not purchased for your use only, then please return to your favorite e-book retailer and purchase your own copy. Thank you for respecting the hard work of this author.

Discover other titles by Cathryn Fox at www.cathrynfox.com. Please sign up for Cathryn's Newsletter for freebies, ebooks, news and contests:
https://app.mailerlite.com/webforms/landing/c1f8n1

ISBN: ebook 978-1-989374-07-8
ISBN print: 978-1-989374-06-1

From my bar stool in Nelly's pub, I scoop my glass up from the long, oaken tabletop and hold it above my head in salute. "Here's to kicking ass and taking numbers," I say to my best friend, the man I call brother, despite the fact that our features are opposite in nearly every single way. Other than our height, and the fact that we both play in the NHL, Kane's longish hair is sun-drenched blond, whereas mine is dark and cropped short. His deep blue eyes have a way of catching the attention of everyone around him. Mine however, with a hint of metal gray, have been compared to an overcast day and help me blend into the background. Being invisible saved my ass a time or two in foster care.

"Here's to coming in first in our division," Kane says as he clinks glasses with me and jabs his thumb into his chest. "The Stanley Cup is coming home to Seattle with us this year, bro," he adds and I swallow half the bubbly soda in one gulp and slam my glass onto the bar top with more force than necessary. The bartender gives me a sideways glance and I grin at him before wiping my mouth with the back of my hand. I glance over my brother's shoulder and take stock of the crowded bar. In the near distance, the shrill of a woman's loud laugh swirls throughout the congested room and mingles with all the other blaring sounds.

Perfume reaches my nose, and as I feed off the energy in the crowd, I let it fuel my blood. I might be the guy to stand back and blend in, but deep down, I'm a total thrill-seeker. Last October however, shortly after the NHL season began, any kind of noise would have sent me to a dark corner drooling like a damn baby. Christ, that concussion really did a number on me. But it wasn't career-ending, and for that I'm grateful. Without hockey, I'm nothing.

"Where the fuck are the rest of the guys?" Kane asks and gestures for another shot.

I laugh but it has no humor. "It's Thursday. Where the fuck do you think they are?" Christ, except for a handful of the guys, most on the team are married with kids, and those who live in Seattle are home snuggled in with their loved ones on this rainy Thursday night. The others are likely holed up in their hotel rooms skyping and babbling shit about missing home. A sound crawls out of my throat, a half laugh, half snort. It's not that I'm jealous of their relationships, or anything. Nope, I'm a bachelor for life, and not fucking jealous at all.

Or much, anyway.

"Right. Pussies," Kane says, his voice a bit slurred. A couple shots of rum will do that to a guy. We have a game in two days, and while Kane can put the booze back as well as the next guy, and still be on top of his game, for me...not so much. I'm not about to risk anything when it comes to hockey. It's all or nothing for me. And I'll only settle for all.

I turn, lean against the bar, and scan the establishment a second time. "We have a live one," I say when I catch sight of the pretty redhead coming from the hallway. She presses her lips together, smoothing her freshly applied color, and runs her hands through her thick, wavy hair. I'm good at reading body language, a must on the ice, and if those gestures aren't a sign that she's open for suggestions, I don't know what is. "Two o'clock," I say and Kane spins on his stool.

"She's gorgeous," he says and I grin when his jaw drops.

I nudge Kane with my shoulder. "Do I know how to pick them for you, or what?"

"You sure you don't want this one? I know you have a thing for redheads."

"Nah. I'm just going to finish my soda and head home. I have some shows to catch up on."

Kane shakes his head and I brace for the lecture. "Are you seriously still watching The Handmaid's Tale?"

"Shut the fuck up, and it wouldn't hurt you to watch something other than sports once in a while."

"Man, you need to get laid more than I thought." He finishes off his drink. "Go ahead. You take this one."

As the girl approaches, I push off the counter and step in front of her. "So I was thinking..." I begin, and she stops abruptly and stares at me with pretty green eyes.

"About?" Her dark lashes fall slowly as her gaze pans the length of me. While she doesn't yet know it, her leisurely inspection of my body is a waste of time. It's not me she's going home with tonight.

"Well, I was thinking about asking for your number." Before I continue, I cringe, and suck in air like I have something nasty on my tongue. "But I have this thing..."

Her eyes narrow in on me. "You have a *thing?*" she asks, and the fact that she's playing along lets me know she's open to a hook-up.

"Yeah, the doctors are calling it a third nipple." I lower my voice and add, "For now, anyway." Kane chuckles as the girl's eyes widen. "More tests need to be done, of course."

She takes a small step backward, like she might catch what I have. "Ah, why are you telling me this?"

I move to the side to make room for my bro, and right on cue, Kane stands. Her gaze shifts, and appreciatively takes in my brother. "Because this guy only has two nipples. You seem like a girl who would appreciate that, plus he told me you were the most beautiful woman in the room."

"He did?" A smile curls up the corners of her mouth, and I inch back even more, biting back my grin as the two begin talking.

And that, ladies and gentlemen, is how to be a good wingman. Not that Kane really needs one, but we have fun playing the game.

Since my job here is done, I plop back down onto my stool and let Kane work his magic. I hang for a bit until Kane pulls his car keys from his pocket and hands them to me.

"Get my car home, bro. We're taking an Uber."

"You got it," I say and finish my soda. I grin at my buddy. "Have fun."

"Take your own advice, why don't you." He stares at me for a moment, like he's truly concerned about my well-being, and I wave my hand to shove him off. He opens his mouth and I snort, turning from him to let him know it's not a conversation we're having. Once he steps away, I angle my head and watch them walk from the bar. When he disappears outside, I pull my phone from my pocket and check the hour. Damn, I put that hook-up together in record time. I'm getting better and better at this shit, and if I hurry, I might be able to catch up on two episodes before I crash.

I grab my glass, about to take my last sip of cola before I head out, when the sound of hands clapping reach my ears. I turn to find a girl nodding and applauding me.

I grin at her. "You liked that, did you?" I ask, as I take in her clear skin, sharp brown eyes that are twinkling with amusement, and dark hair tied back in a ponytail. My gaze drops to her loose-fitting scrubs.

"Yeah, well played. Does your charm only work on girls, or does it work on guys too?"

I arch a brow and cock my head as my gaze moves over her make-up free face. Not that she needs paint. She has that whole girl-next-door thing going on and it really works for her. "You don't strike me as the kind of girl looking for a hook-up."

She gives a very unladylike snort as I finish my last gulp of soda. "What?" She tugs on her hair. "Is it the ponytail, or the fact that I'm not showing my tits?"

Her retort catches me off guard and I nearly choke on my drink as my gaze drops to her chest. "Uh, yeah," I say, instantly liking her. The truth is, women approach me all the time, and while I seem to have an instant rapport with this one, and there's an undeniable spark between us, she didn't come over here to get me between her sheets and no way is she really looking for me to be her wingman. So, what does she want?

She laughs at that. "At least you're honest." Dark eyes full of curiosity and playfulness narrow in on me, but behind those dark lashes I sense her cautiousness. "What else gave me away?"

"You're dressed in scrubs."

She shrugs. "I'm a nurse at Seattle General. I came here straight from work to meet a friend for drinks."

"You have freckles," I say, that observation coming out of nowhere and catching her off guard.

She crinkles her nose. "Yeah, I know. They're awful."

"I never said they were awful."

She rolls her eyes like she doesn't believe me. "Well, you have a dimple."

I poke my finger into my right cheek. "Wait, you say that

like it's a bad thing?"

She sighs. "It's not."

I lean toward her conspiratorially. "I'm a nice guy, and because I am, I'm going to give you a warning. If you look at it too long, you'll be forever charmed."

"Oh, my God. Are you for real?"

"Sadly yes," I say, and she laughs with me. I glance around. "Where's this friend you're having drinks with? Is she going to hate me for keeping you captive with my dimple?"

"Ah, nope." She casts a sad glance at the door. "She kind of left with your friend."

Oh shit. "Ah, sorry about that."

"Yeah, that was Lindsay. My best friend."

"And now I'm responsible for you drinking by yourself?"

"I'm done drinking. I have a shift tomorrow." She glances around. "She's safe with your friend, right?"

"Absolutely. Kane is one of the good guys."

She nods. "Okay, so I really am curious. Do your lines only work only on women, or do they work on guys too?"

I gesture for the bartender for two more sodas. "Want to find out?"

"Sure. It's not like I have anything better to do."

"Okay. What's your type?"

"You know, the typical, tall dark and handsome." She holds her hand out. "I'm Jules, by the way. You should probably know that much if you're going to be my wingman."

"Rider," I say and take her soft hand in to mine. Damn, her hands are so tiny. Much like the rest of her. After a quick shake, I scan the bar. "What about that guy there?"

"Too much hair gel," she says. "If he moved in for a kiss, it might put my eye out."

I grin. "Okay, what about that one?"

She crinkles her nose. "He hasn't looked up from his phone all night."

"Yeah, he'd probably want you to send boob picture or something." I eye her teasingly. "Wait, are you into that? Asking for a friend."

She laughs and whacks me. "No."

"What about him?" I spot a nice-looking guy—hey, I'm man enough to admit when a guy is good looking—cuts across the floor, his gaze locked on the bartender, and from the interest in his eyes, I'm not certain it's a drink he wants from the man. Nothing wrong with that, but if she's interested, it's still not going to stop me from being a good wingman.

"Yeah, he's kind of cute."

I stand, and cut him off. "Hey, bud," I begin. "I've got to get out of here." I jerk my thumb toward Jules. "I don't want to leave my friend Jules alone." The dude looks around my shoulder to take in Jules as she twists on the stool. "We're just friends because she's not my type."

Recognition flashes in the guy's eyes when they stray back to me. "Wait, aren't you—?" he begins, and I cut him off by holding my hands in front of myself, like I'm about to cup two perfect breasts. I get it, he's a fan, and while I'm always up for a picture or an autograph, I don't want to switch gears right now. I realize I'm loved because of hockey, but I guess I just want to be me right now. Not that anyone loves that guy.

"Her tits you know. They're way too big. I'm a mouthful kind of guy."

Jules squeals in horror behind me, and I bite back a grin as the dude stares at me like I'm a serial killer trying to lure him to my basement with the help of my girlfriend. He gestures with a nod to the group of guys behind him. "Uh, yeah, I have to go."

Jules and I burst out laughing as he zig-zags through the crowd and meets up with his friends. They huddle and cast suspicious glances our way. Maybe it's time for us to vacate the place. I reserve my fighting for the rink.

Jules gives a slow shake of her head. "You've got no game, Rider."

"Hey, I've got game," I say, feigning offense. "That guy was just more interested in the bartender. Let me try again," I say, although oddly enough, I've lost the desire to hook her up with some random guy.

She gives me a dubious look, stands, and shoves me. "Move aside, rookie. Let me show you how it's done." She scans the room. "What's your type? And yeah, I get it. You don't like big breasts."

"I never said that," I counter as I try to judge the size of hers, but they're hidden so well behind her scrubs I can't tell. "I like *all* breasts."

She puckers her lips. "I bet you do."

"Yeah. I do," I admit and she shakes her head. "What can I say? I'm honest to a fault." When she rolls her eyes, I say, "I like women, Jules. Tall, short, thin, plump. You name it."

"Hair color?"

I glance at her ponytail. "As long as I can tug it, it doesn't matter what color it is."

As soon as the words leave my mouth, her lips part, and wait...was that a fast intake of breath I just heard? I study her closely, examine the fresh flush on her face. Funny, others might find her plain, but the more time I spend with her, the cuter I find those freckles, and the sexier I find everything about her—including her scrubs. I can't even blame it on alcohol since I'm dry tonight. Yeah, okay, maybe Kane was right. I need to get laid more often.

"Did I embarrass you?" I ask.

"No," she says, with a quick jerk of her head.

I part my legs on the stool and since I value my nuts, I

resist the urge to pull her between them. "Then why are your cheeks red?"

She lets out an exasperated breath. "Do you say everything that pops into your brain?"

"Pretty much." My gaze moves over her pretty pink cheeks. "Oh, wait, maybe you're not embarrassed. Maybe you're arous—"

"So you don't have a type," she blurts out, cutting me off. "How about the one coming toward you right now. Twelve o'clock."

I look the pretty girl over. Perfect hair. Perfect makeup. Perfect clothes. "She seems very high maintenance."

"Yeah, I think you might be right."

"Hmmm, what about that one?" she says and I follow the direction she's pointing.

I give a slow shake of my head. "Nope, she's downing her drinks like she fears there's going to be an alcohol shortage."

"What about her friend?"

I study her body language for a second. "See the way she's scanning the place, her hands braced by her sides?"

"Yeah," she says.

"I'm pretty sure she fears we're about to face a zombie apocalypse."

Jules laughs out loud and when it dies off, she says, "What about the one coming right at you."

I reluctantly tear my gaze from Jules and make eye contact with the blonde. I stiffen. Shit. I know where this is going, and I'm not in the mood—not when I've been having a good time here.

"What's wrong?" Jules asks.

"Nothing," I lie.

"I thought that was you, Rider," the girl says, and puts her hands on my chest as she juts one hip out in a suggestive manner.

"Do I know you?" While I might not know her, I know her type, and I know what she's after. But what's really bugging me is Jules and I were having fun, and I wasn't ready for that to end. Honestly, I haven't laughed or joked like that with a woman in...ever.

The blonde gives a breathless laugh. "Not yet." She runs her finger down my chest. "I'm Candy, by the way."

"Of course you are," I say.

"Want to get out of here? Go back to my place, or yours if you prefer."

Wow, how fucking rude to act like Jules doesn't even exist. Sure, she's not the kind of girl usually found on my arm, but still.

"Candy, this is Jules. My fiancée." I tap my leg, a gesture for Jules to take a seat.

Without even missing a beat, Jules takes my cue, sidles closer to me, and extends her hand. "Candy, it's nice to meet you." Goddammit, a woman with beauty and brains. If I weren't a one-night kind of guy, I'd hang on tight to this one. But I'm not into tomorrows, so that's a stupid thought.

Candy falters and stares at Jules' hand like it's about to grow a head and bite her.

"Yeah right," she fires back, her eyes narrowing as her head bobs back and forth between the two of us.

"Why is that so hard to believe?" Jules asks in a voice so sultry and smooth it could churn butter.

Candy's head jerks back, her lips pursed so tight they're beginning to turn white. "Rider Lewis, the NHL's best wing-man, does not date, or do commitments. Everyone knows that."

In a move that displays possession, Jules settles between my spread legs and sets her sweet ass down on my left thigh.

She blinks innocently at Candy. "I guess I must have missed the memo."

JULES

As we maneuver through the bar, I angle my head and take in Rider's cute dimple. "Why are you grinning at me like that?"

"Like what?"

"Like you hit the boards one too many times."

Rider opens the heavy front door and gestures for me to exit. "Hockey fan, are you?" he asks as he joins me on the wet sidewalk.

I snort. "Not even a little bit."

"Are you serious?" He gives a slow shake of his head, and runs his fingers through his short hair. "I don't think we can be friends any more, Jules."

"We're friends now, are we?" I ask.

He gestures with a nod. "It's over, and I'm afraid you're going to have to walk on the other side of the street."

I whack his stomach—damn, the man is hard—and he lets loose a loud oomph.

"For the record," he says, "I'm not a fan of nurses either."

"What could you possibly have against nurses?" I hold my

hand out and test the skies. Looks like the rain has stopped. For now. I mean, this is Seattle and it could downpour again any second.

"Last year I landed in the hospital—"

"What were you in the hospital for?"

"Nothing important," he says quickly, and continues with, "As soon as I'd drift off, the damn nurses would wake me up. It was fucking annoying. Then they'd poke and stick me with things and I think they took great pleasure in it. Sadistic, all of you."

I laugh. "Aw, did the nurses upset the little baby with three nipples?"

He scrunches up his face. "Funny girl." He gives my pony-tail a tug and the second he does, the air around us shifts, becomes a little more volatile...electric. My lips part, and his gaze drops, like he can't take his eyes from my mouth. Okay, I must be imagining things here. Lindsay is the kind of girl who attracts guys like Rider and Kane. Where she's adventurous, bold and always up for something wild, I'm the quiet girl, the caretaker, the good girl who always blends into the wood-work. Tonight, the fact that Rider chose Lindsay—not me—for his friend Kane, is a testament to that.

"So...ah. Yeah," Rider says, shoving his hands into the pockets of his jeans. "You never got to show me how it was done."

"How...what was done?" I ask, my mind careening off in an erotic direction, imagining all the dirty things we could show each other. Which makes me nearly laugh. What dirty things do I know?

"You called me a rookie when I was trying to find you a guy, and said you'd show me how it was done. You never got a chance to be my wingman."

"Right, and it's wingwoman."

He nudges me with his shoulder, and the intimate contact

sends a ridiculous streak of heat through my chilled body. "What did you think I meant?"

"That," I say quickly. Too quickly judging by his smirk. With a little more confidence I add, "That's what I thought you meant." His grin widens, like he's a cocky son of a bitch who knows my stupid brain had gone off in a dirty direction.

"What would you have said?" he asks.

"It was a gem. I'm going to save it for next time."

"Oh, we're doing this again, are we? I thought you said you didn't like hockey players."

I actually said I didn't like hockey, not hockey players. Truthfully, I've never met a hockey player until tonight. But instead of pointing that out, I say, "And you don't like nurses, so we're even. And...you did ruin my date night with my girlfriend, so I feel like you owe me date."

"You want to go on a date?"

"Not with you," I say, and make a face like the idea is absurd. I pull my phone from my pocket, about to grab an Uber, even though it's still early and the thought of going home to an empty apartment doesn't hold the appeal it did an hour ago. Normally I love the quiet after a busy shift. Love to make a hot cup of herbal tea and whip up dinner for one in the kitchen.

"What are you doing?" he asks, and cocks his head to the side as he stares at my phone.

"Getting an Uber and going home."

He shakes his friend's keys. "I can drive you. Seeing you home safely is the least I can do after setting your girlfriend up with my brother."

I lower my phone. "Wait. Kane is your brother?" My God, the two look nothing alike. I never would have put that together. But damn, their parents must be proud to have two professional hockey players in the family.

"Not by blood, but yeah." He quickly turns from me, but

not before I catch the flash of darkness in his eyes. Why do I suddenly get the feeling that I touched on a sore spot? He holds the fob out, presses it, and in the near distance a car door unlocks.

"Well, I have four siblings. I'm the oldest of five." Why the hell did I just tell him that?

He turns back to me, and he has the strangest look on his face. I'm not sure what to make of it, and I don't know him well enough to call it, but for the briefest of seconds I get the impression that he's all alone in this world. But he's not. He has Kane, and his entire team, right?

"That's nice," he says so quietly I have to strain to hear.

Silence falls over us, and I suddenly can't remember what we were talking about before I asked about his brother. When he shifts from one foot to the other, the keys rattle.

Right, he'd offered me a ride home, before my brain went off in another direction.

"I don't get into cars with strangers," I say with a lift of my chin.

Humor is back in his eyes when he turns to me. "Friends with every Uber driver in Seattle, are you?" he teases, that sexy little dimple on display again.

I give an exaggerated eye roll that seems to amuse him. "Well no. Of course not, but they have safety measures. You could be a serial killer, for all I know."

"I'm not and I don't make it a habit of driving random women home either, you know. Maybe you're not a real nurse." He glances the length of me. "Maybe you only wear scrubs because you're an organ thief and it saves time when you're ready to harvest some unsuspecting dude's parts," he teases, as he cups his crotch.

I burst out laughing. "You have a very wild imagination. I'm not after your organs, Rider." I point downward. "Especially that one."

"Whew. Okay, what do you do for fun?" he questions, like he's not ready for this night to be over any more than I am.

"I like gardening, and art, and I like to repair and paint old furniture." I'm about to ask him what he does for fun, but he slaps his head.

"What a coincidence."

I fold my arms, and stare at him, wondering where he's going with this, but entertained with his antics just the same. "What?"

He jerks his thumb down the street. "I was actually on my way to get a whopper wiener at the Bad Art Museum. Join me. We can eat and look at art."

"Bad art, you mean."

"Beauty is in the eye of the beholder, baby."

"And those wieners will kill you. Instead of whopper wiener, they should be called heart attack hotdog."

He laughs at the joke. "So you want one, too?"

"Well, yeah."

He laughs harder and I join in as we start down the sidewalk. "After we eat, if you decide I'm not a serial killer, and my intentions are to get you home safely, I'll drive you. If you're still not comfortable, I'll get you an Uber."

"Deal."

Light rain drops sprinkle down on us. "We better make a run for it," he says. "This isn't looking good."

He captures my hand, and we hurry down the sidewalk, but the light rain turns to fat drops and soaks our clothes before we reach our destination.

We're drenched and laughing by the time we step inside the Bad Art Museum. "I can't remember the last time I was here," I say, blinking against the glare of the orange wall, the color resembling that of a Cheeto. "Were you really planning on coming here tonight? Be honest."

"I'm always honest."

"I get that about you."

"And no, I wasn't." His head dips, and that's when I realize my scrubs are drenched and stuck to my body. I pull on my top and it makes a sucking sound as it breaks the bond with my flesh.

"Average size," he says under his breath. "I think that's my favorite."

"Rider!" I burst out and his eyes cut to mine. "Are you talking about my breasts?"

"Yeah," he says, not a hint of embarrassment about him.

"You need to get some filters, my friend," I say, even though I sort of like that he says what he's thinking. There are no games with this one, and honestly, it's a refreshing break. Not that I'm looking for anything more from him. I'm not looking for a relationship, and according to Candy, he doesn't do relationships. Yeah, sure, he might like my *average* breasts, but I'm average all over, and that puck bunny...she was hands down, over-the-top gorgeous. No way can I compare to the women who throw themselves at him. Nor do I want to. Being his friend, however... that sounds nice.

"Now let's eat and look at art." I follow him to the counter and let my gaze drop to take in the way his low-slung jeans cradle his impressive ass. I don't think the man is a serial killer, but damn, he has a killer body. In my line of work, I've seen many naked men over the years, but I have a feeling I've not seen Rider's kind of naked.

He orders two whopper wieners and two drinks. I reach for my purse and he stops me. "This heart attack is on me."

"Fine, I buy next time, and I get to pick where we go."

"At least I know you eat meat, and you're not going to force me to go someplace where they serve weeds and twigs."

"You don't strike me as the kind of guy who can be forced to do anything you don't want to do."

"I kind of get that same vibe from you, too." As I bask in the compliment, he pays and hands me a can of soda and a hotdog. I grab two paper straws and make my way to the table, but he stops at the condiments. He pours so much mustard on his dog, it's spilling everywhere.

"Would you like a wiener to go with that mustard?" I ask, and make a face that showcases my disgust.

He shrugs, uncaring. "What can I say? I like mustard."

"The bacon, cheese, chilis, and onions don't cut it?"

He swipes at the dripping mustard from his bun and puts his finger into his mouth. "Nope."

I give a slow shake of my head. "The things I'm learning about you tonight."

I slide into a puffy purple booth and he sits across from me. My stomach grumbles loudly, reminding me I skipped dinner. Rider arches a brow when the sound reaches his ears.

"Work was insane tonight. Sometimes I don't get a chance to eat." I bite into my hot dog and as I chew, a moan crawls into my throat. I briefly shut my eyes and when I open them again, I find Rider staring at me, his hot dog poised in his hand, inches from his mouth.

"What?" I ask and grab a napkin. "Do I have food on my face or something?"

"Yeah," he says, the black in his gorgeous eyes bleeding into that strange shade of gray. For the first time since I met him, I'm get the sense he's *not* saying what's really going through his brain.

Deciding I want to know him better, I ask, "What do you do for fun, besides pick up women for your brother? Wait, why do you do that, anyway? Kane doesn't look like he needs any help getting his own girls."

He causally rolls one shoulder. "He doesn't." He licks more mustard from his fingers, and my God, I'm not sure what is going on with me, but what he's doing should not be one bit sexy. No, it's an excellent way to transmit diseases and infections. While my brain fully understands that, the needy juncture between my legs doesn't much care. Yeah, that damn traitorous juncture is quite enthralled with his mouth, the sucking sounds he's making and how those lips of his would feel...

"Fuck that's good," he says, and my thoughts come crashing back to the present. "And you're right. Kane doesn't need help with the ladies. It's just a game we play."

"Does it work the other way around?" I crack my soda and slide my straw in. "Does he come in as your wingman?"

"Not really."

"You like girls, right?" I bite, and chew and add, "I mean, it's okay if you don't."

He laughs. "Yeah, I like girls. I told you that already. I like all girls, all shapes and all sizes."

"But you're not into hook-ups?"

Mustard pools on his plate and he dips the end of his hot dog into it. "It's hockey season. I keep my focus on the game. I don't let anything distract me."

"Like alcohol or women." He arches a brow and I continue with, "You ordered us both a soda at the bar after I said I was done drinking, and I'm guessing that's what was in your glass before I arrived. And that woman, Candy," I say drawing out her name. "She was an easy mark, Rider. I bet she had a bullseye right here," I say, and twist in the stool to point to the small of my back.

Rider laughs. "What about you? Are you into hook-ups?"

"Not really."

"Then why did you want me to be your wingman?"

"I can talk to a guy, but it doesn't mean I'm going to go home with him, you know." He frowns and takes another big bite of his hot dog, nearly devouring half of it already. "What? Is that a foreign concept to you, or something?" He looks upward as he chews, like he's thinking hard on that. "Oh, I get it. Puck bunnies. God's gift to hockey players."

He nods, and takes a drink of his soda to wash down his food. "What about you? Every guy's fantasy is to walk into the bedroom to find his woman dressed in a naughty nurse uniform."

"Not yours, though, right?" I take a pull from my straw. "You know, seeing as you don't like nurses."

"That's right." He's about to take a drink and stops, his eyes widening. "Wait. Do you have one of those outfits?"

"No, I don't have one, and even if I did, I wouldn't wear something so ridiculous."

"I don't think it's ridiculous. A lot of guys are into that kind of thing. You must have a ton of *scrub bunnies* after you."

"Scrub bunnies? That's not even a thing, Rider. You're insane."

"What would you call them?" he asks as he kicks his legs out to get comfortable, his feet touching mine under the table. Why the hell does every touch feel so electric?

"I don't think guys are bunnies. Maybe hounds."

His cute grin is back. "Hospital hounds?"

"Yeah, that's more like it. Candy said you don't do relationships," I say switching subjects as I glance at the big velvet picture of Elvis adorning the wall beside me. "Is that just for hockey season, or are you a sworn bachelor for life?"

"Aren't you full of questions tonight." Like we've done it a hundred times before, he reaches out and swipes his thumb over the corner of my mouth. "You're the messiest eater."

"I am not. You are. You've got mustard all over your face. You look like a big Cheeto. You're going to blend in with the walls soon."

He grins and, my God, I want to touch that dimple. "You think I'm big?"

I laugh. Hard. "Really?" I shake my head. "That's what you took from that?"

"Sworn bachelor for life," he admits. "What about you?"

"Right guy just hasn't come along yet?" Or maybe he has, and my regimented ways, the fact that I always try to control my emotions and my surroundings, sent him packing.

Loosen up once in a while, will you.

As my ex's words ping around my brain—words he'd spoken to me in the bedroom—Rider looks at me long and hard. "Ever been serious?"

I shake all thoughts of Jason from my brain. "Ah, not really." With the long day taking its toll on me, topped off by the food coma I'm now suffering, a yawn I have no control over rumbles in my throat.

Rider grins. "Am I boring you?"

I cover my mouth and shake my head. No woman could ever be bored in his presence. I know I'm not. "No. Sorry. It's been a long night."

"How about I take you home?" He pulls the keys from his pocket. "Kane owns a Ferrari 306 Spider, and I can get you home super-fast." A fine shiver goes through me and he angles his head, those astute eyes of his assessing me. "Wait, I take it you're not a thrill seeker like me."

I crinkle my nose, as my stomach tightens at the thought of flying down the street at supersonic speed. As a nurse, I see the results of such speed, see far too much loss. Perhaps that's why I'm so cautious and controlled. "Sort of the complete opposite."

His gaze moves over my face again, then lowers for a low sweep of my damp top. "No worries, Jules," he says in a low voice that makes me wonder if it's normally reserved for the pillow. "I can go slow. Real slow."

Honest to God, if I didn't know better—and I do—the soft way he just said *slow* makes me think he's talking about sex, and not getting behind the wheel of a fast car. Okay, clearly, I'm exhausted and hallucinating, right?

3

RIDER

I'm in a good mood. A damn good mood, and I'm not sure why. I mean, there's no reason for me to be upset or angry. We just kicked the shit out of the Anaheim team, which means we're one step closer to securing the cup, but I'm not entirely sure that's where my high is coming from. I lift my stick as I glide across the ice, and the crowd goes crazy, cheers erupting from the stands. Some very familiar puck bunnies jump up and down and wave home-made banners to fight for our attention.

I get checked from behind and turn to see Kane. "You going to hit that?" he says to me, gesturing with a nod to some blonde as she screams my name at the top of her lungs.

"Nah, not tonight."

"I'm starting to worry about you, dude," he says as we make our way off the ice and into the locker room where the energy is high and everyone is talking about Zander's winning goal. My gaze goes to Zander, and while he's all smiles, he's on the phone, a big grin on his face. Since he got married to Sam, and now they're bringing another child into the world, a sibling for his daughter Daisy, I've never seen the man happier.

"You know my rules. No sex during game week."

"Game's over for the week," Kane informs me. "We don't play again until next week in Philly."

"Yeah, okay so maybe I'll hit that," I say just to get my bro off my back. But the truth is, Jules has been on my mind since I first met her. I'd driven her home, but we didn't exchange numbers. Kane probably didn't get her friend's number either, as he rarely—or never—goes out with the same woman twice. I need to forget her. I want to forget her. So why the fuck can't I get her smile out of my goddamn head?

I grin, and Kane must mistake it, because he says, "Now look at you. Sex is putting a smile back on your face."

Before I can stop myself, I say, "Let's get a drink at Nelly's first." Shit what am I doing? Hoping to run into Jules again? I mean the odds of that... Actually, I don't know what the odds are. I have no idea how often she goes there. It's close to her work, but still.

Kane shakes off his gloves and gives me the side eye. "Why do you want to go back there?"

"No reason."

I try to shift away from his watchful eyes. Dammit, I wish my brother couldn't read me so well. Then again, I suppose I can read him too. Fifteen years ago, at the age of fourteen, I moved in with his family of five, and Kane and I shared a room. I was only supposed to be there temporarily, but we totally hit it off like brothers—which meant we bickered about everything and anything. Maybe I was resentful that he had a loving family and stability, and I think he hated that he had to share everything with the asshole who'd just invaded his home, and it's possible I was a real asshole. But then one day, a group of guys thought it would be fun to kick the shit out of the poor kid from the wrong side of the tracks, a kid who did not belong in their middle-class neighborhood—or so they thought.

Like any good brother, Kane came running to my defense, and back to back, he stood with me, fought with me. I'll never forget that day. My heart still wobbles a little when I think about it. We'd been on our way to the rink and I was lagging behind. Kane was a kick-ass hockey player by the time I met him. I was a nobody. But his parents bought me a pair of skates—maybe they thought it would help us bond. No one really won the fight that day, and those fucking douche bags ran away with my skates, but it did change things between Kane and me. A truce had been formed when he lent me his skates for tryouts, and while I never really threw myself in to anything back then, I wanted to make Kane proud of me. I ended up impressing everyone, and earned myself a spot on the junior team. In the end, I showed a tremendous amount of skill and I guess that's why Kane's parents never shipped me off to the next home. With hockey, I was worthy of being loved. I was someone.

"You sure about that?" Kane asks, bringing my thoughts back. "Absolutely no reason you want to go back to Nelly's?"

"Yeah, why?"

"I don't know. I'm the one usually dragging you to the bars. Did you hook up with someone after I left? Wait, I thought I saw Candy in the parking lot with all her friends when I grabbed an Uber."

"I saw her, too." I tug off my helmet and run my hands through my wet hair. "But we didn't hook up. I ended up talking to Lindsay's friend." When Kane stands there, his look stunned as he stares at me, confusion all over his face, I say, "Lindsay. You know, the girl you left with?"

"I know who she is." He drops down onto the bench and tugs off his skates. "How do you know her name?"

I shrug like it's nothing. "Jules, her friend told me. They

met for drinks, but I ruined her night."

"It's not like you to ruin a girl's night." Kane grins. "Maybe you really are out of practice."

"Ha. Ha. Jules had just gotten off work at the hospital. She's a nurse, and was having a drink with her friend when I intervened."

"And you didn't sleep with her?"

"No."

"How did you learn so much about her, then?"

"It's called talking," I say, deflecting so I don't have to think too hard on why I was interested in learning so much about her. "You can do that with girls. You should try it."

"Yeah, Lindsay and I talked, too. She makes pottery." He gives me a wink. "She's very good with her hands." I roll my eyes at him, and he feigns offence. "What? I mean it. She owns a store and showed me her pieces online. She's really talented."

I eye my bro. Is he messing with me? It's not like him to connect with a woman outside the bedroom? "You're kidding me."

"Nope." I stare at his face, but there is nothing in his expression to suggest he's lying.

"Well anyway, Jules was a bit pissed that I sent her friend away with you, so we grabbed a hotdog and I drove her home."

Kane strips and reaches for his towel. "Are you sure that's all you did?" he presses. Okay, so maybe I'm not known for my verbal skills, and yeah, she had a killer body, with perfect breasts I could really sink my teeth into. Fuck knows, I've thought about it. A lot. I thought about it while tugging my dick in the shower, crawling into bed at night, and climbing from it in the morning. Jesus, when her shirt stuck to her like a second skin, saliva dripped from the corners of my mouth. Good thing I was wet from the rain, otherwise I might have scared her off. Christ, maybe I should have slept with her. Then again, she's not the type to just jump into bed with a man. Not that there is anything wrong with that. A woman should own her sexuality, and be able to do what she wants, with who she wants—as long as she's safe. But Jules straight up told me she wasn't into hook-ups.

I ignore Kane's inquisitive glare and make my way to the showers. The hot water scalds my skin and I bask in it, hoping it does double duty. One, I need it to wash away the sweat of the game, and two, I need it to douse the memories of Jules that keep plaguing me.

"Actually, I was planning on hitting up Nelly's tonight, anyway," Kane says, grabbing the shower next to me. "I'm just surprised you brought it up first."

I shampoo my hair and angle my head. "Yeah, what's going on?"

"Lindsay is going to be there. Apparently, it's karaoke night. She likes to sing."

Now it's my turn to stare at him like I'm stunned. "You're going to meet the same girl twice, and listen to her sing?"

He rolls one shoulder. "Sure, why not."

My head dips and I slowly shake it. "Who are you and what have you done with my brother?"

He laughs. "Jules will probably be with her," he says, his gaze boring into me. "Wait, that's what you said her name was right?"

Don't react, Rider.

Don't fucking react.

"Yeah, whatever," I say, but from the half laugh, half snort that just escaped Kane's mouth, I'm not sure he bought it and I'm seriously wondering what the fuck is wrong with me, too. Candy was right. I don't do relationships. Ever. I'm not good at them and I'm definitely not good enough for a girl like Jules, who likely comes from a close-knit family that sits around and has Sunday dinners. I'm a guy from the streets, tossed and kicked around for years. Unwanted. Unlovable. No, I'm not throwing a fucking pity party, here. It's just the facts. But I have my hockey, and I'm loved for that, and that's enough for me.

I rinse my hair and body and keep my movements casual as I head back to the change room. Although, I can't deny that I'm looking forward to seeing Jules again. She was fun to be around. Maybe tonight she'll play my wingwoman and show the rookie how it's done. I laugh at that, and Kane steps up beside me.

"Something funny?"

"I was just thinking about something...Never mind," I say, not wanting to give him any more fuel.

I check the time, and tug on my clothes.

"I have to stop at Jaclyn's before we go," Kane says.

"The kids okay?" I ask.

"Cameron made me something at school, and he wants to show it to me."

My heart misses a stupid beat. Kane is close to both of his younger sisters and their kids—hell so am I, even though I'm not really the kids' uncle—and it's nice that Cameron made something for Rider. I'm not fucking jealous at all.

"You okay bro?" Kane asks and slaps me on the back.

"Yeah, good."

"You're coming with me. The kids want to see you too."

"Yeah?"

He whacks me on the back of the head. "Of course. Don't be stupid."

After we put our gear away, we hike our hockey bags over our shoulders and walk through a pack of women on the way to Kane's car. He usually drives us everywhere—he's loving his new car—so when we're in Seattle, my Jeep rarely leaves my garage. We make our way across town, and enter suburbia where all the houses are similar and all the lawns neatly mowed. There are kids bikes in the driveway and numerous toys on manicured lawns. It's a nice place to raise a family.

We hurry up the walkway and Kane rings the bell about ten times. "Maybe I should let us in." He reaches into his pocket for his key, but the door flings open, and my head rears back as I take in Jaclyn's frazzled state. Her long hair is a tousled mess, her clothes have food stains and her cheeks are red like she's been running a marathon. With three rambunctious kids under five, I supposed that's comparable.

I reach a hand out and stop midair. "Ah, I think you have a noodle in your hair," I say and she rolls her eyes and tugs it free.

"Yup, there it is." She glances over her shoulder. "Kids, Uncle Kane and Rider are here." Footsteps pound on the floor behind her, and she gives us both a fast hug. "Sorry I didn't catch the game live. Caleb is away on business, as you know, and the sitter bailed earlier." She glances over her shoulder as three kids come running. Cameron, the oldest of the three, is in kindergarten, and the twins, Carly and Carter, are toddlers. "I don't blame her," she says under her breath. "These guys are a handful."

"If you ever need a break," Kane says.

"You'll watch them?" she asks, her big blue eyes hopeful.

"Well, I was thinking Rider here could since he has lots of spare time." He gives me a knowing wink. "He doesn't seem to be doing much on his days off."

She narrows her eyes and glares at her brother. "And you're too busy on your days off." She holds her hands up. "I don't want details, but if I see one more picture of you and some bunny in the paper." She takes a deep breath and lets it out slowly. "It's time you find yourself a nice girl and settle down." She pokes her finger in to Kane's chest, then into mine. "You too."

I laugh at that. "Not going to be happen, but I'd be happy to help you out. Although I don't know anything about kids." I do, however, know someone who does. Whoa! Why the hell did that thought pop into my brain? Jules grew up the oldest of four, but I'm not about to ask her to babysit with me. Maybe I'm not quite over that concussion from last fall. It's the only logical explanation for my ridiculous thoughts.

Carly sits on my foot and wraps her little legs around mine. Carter jumps on the other one, while Cameron grab's Rider's hand.

"We want a ride. We want a ride," Carly says, and my damn legs are so tired from the game, it takes effort, but I'm not about to disappoint them. I walk down the hallway and they squeal as we enter the kitchen. I go still when I see Cameron showing Kane the picture stuck to the fridge.

"He had to draw his family and wanted to show you guys," Jaclyn says.

My heart misses a beat and I suck in a breath to restart it when I see that I'm standing next to Kane, a hockey stick in my hand.

"I'm in it," I say under my breath.

Jaclyn whacks my stomach. "Of course you're in it, stupid."

"Why is everyone calling me stupid tonight, and hitting me?" I say, even though I'm not upset.

"Stupid, stupid, stupid," Carly and Carter begin chanting as they rock against my feet, wanting to be carried around and letting me know in no uncertain terms I'm not living up to my end of being the uncle.

"That's not a nice word," Jaclyn scolds with a wave of her finger, and my jaw drops open.

"Exactly," I say, and she whacks me again.

I let out a loud oomph and get her in a head-lock to run my knuckles over her hair. She squeals and the kids all laugh.

"Say uncle," I say.

"Uncle!" the kids all yell, and I let Jaclyn go. She works to smooth her hair down and I stop her. "Don't. I think I improved it."

She gives me the death glare, one she perfected at eleven, and reaches for the kids. "Okay guys, leave Uncle Rider alone. He's tired after his game."

She picks them off my feet and they dash into the other room. I pull out a chair as Kane tells Cameron how much he likes the picture. "Why did you draw Rider bigger than me, though?" he asks and flexes his biceps. "I'm much bigger."

Cameron laughs, and flexes his arms, mimicking his uncle. "Daddy says I'm strong."

I squeeze his bicep. "These are bigger than Uncle Kane's," I tease and Kane throws me a challenging glare.

"Don't hate me cause the ladies like me better, bro," he says.

"Okay, on that note time to get ready for bed, Cameron," Jaclyn says. "Give your uncles a hug and go brush up."

After Cameron dashes off, Jaclyn says, "Thanks for stopping by. I know you guys are busy, but the kids have been missing you." A bang sounds from the other room and she winces. "I think I need to check that out."

Kane checks his phone. "No worries we need to get going anyway."

"The next time I see you guys, I want to hear that you've both found nice girls and are finally settling down. You're both getting too old for the lifestyles you're living."

"Rider is the oldest, so he should be thinking—" Kane begins and turns to me.

I laugh and punch him on the shoulder, but the laugh is to cover what I'm really feeling. I *am* tired of this fucking lifestyle. Maybe I do want what the others have. I just...well, it's just not something that's going to happen for me.

4

JULES

I glance around the busy bar as Lindsay walks up to the stage to put her name in for karaoke. She has a great voice, and is talented in so many ways. If I sang, I'd clear the place out quicker than a smoke bomb. The only time my friend ever got me up to sing was when I had too many shots of tequila after a very rough night at the hospital. Tequila and I don't mix, apparently. Which is why I now avoid it at all costs. I don't like it when I'm not in control of myself.

Lindsay comes back to the table, and a couple of guys at the bar look like they're about to approach, but she turns her back to them, giving me her undivided attention—probably to make up for abandoning me the other night. She sits across from me and flashes a smile that has 'truce' written all over it. But I'm not mad that she bailed. Heck, why not go have a good time with Kane? If she hadn't left, then I never would have met Rider.

Rider.

Good God, why the hell can't I stop thinking about him? He's a distraction I don't need, and even a few of the nurses asked me if I was okay, when they found me daydreaming. I'd only spent a few hours with the guy. Did he really leave that much of an impression?

Yeah, he kind of did.

"So tell me more about Kane," I press, wanting to get my mind on something else. I'd only arrived a few minutes ago and snagged the corner table in the busy bar. My shift ended later than I would have like—there was a horrible motorcycle accident and I stayed to help out. Afterward, for some unknown reason, I ran home to change and freshen up before meeting Lindsay for drinks. Okay, okay, maybe I do know the real reason for acting out of character. Maybe somewhere in the back of my brain I thought I might run in to Rider again, and wanted to look a little more put together. I usually turn the TV on for background noise when I'm home alone, but I found myself flicking through the stations looking for tonight's game. I don't normally watch sports of any kind, and I wasn't lying when I said I wasn't a hockey fan, so why I found myself switching stations to find the game, and then planting my ass on the sofa to watch is beyond me.

"He was really nice, and was actually interested in my pottery." She shakes her phone. "His eyes didn't glaze over when I showed him pictures."

I laugh at that. I always enjoy hearing her stories and while I'm neither spontaneous or reckless, I do love living vicariously through her. "He clearly has good taste."

"He mentioned something about his mother and her upcoming birthday."

My lids pop open. "He talked about his mother? Are you serious?"

"Sounds like he comes from a close family. Anyway, I think he wants to get her a few pieces." She cocks her head, and gives me a dreamy smile. "Isn't that nice?"

"It's really nice," I say as I consider Kane's family. Rider calls him brother, but they're obviously not blood-related. Does Rider have a family of his own? A mother, a father, blood siblings?

"Are you falling for him already?" I ask, my stomach churning uneasily. Hockey players are known for their wild ways—I can't forget what Candy said about Rider—and I don't want my friend to get hurt.

"Of course not. He just seemed really...nice."

Oh no, she *is* falling for him.

"Rider said he was one of the good guys," I say. I really hope it's true and he's not stringing my friend along. She's a girl who puts herself out there, wears her heart on her sleeve, and despite numerous bad break-ups and scars that run deep, she continues to step out of her comfort zone. She can tell me it's about personal growth all she wants, but I avoid vulnerability at all cost, and nothing or no one is going to change that.

"Rider?"

"Yeah, his friend. You know, the guy who told you he had a third nipple." I chuckle softly. "Remember him?" God, why is it I want to talk about him, to just say his name?

Lindsay's perfectly manicured brows arch, and her green eyes narrow in on me as she runs a curly lock of red hair around her finger. I fiddle with my own hair, which is still in a ponytail. I might have washed up, put on a clean pair of jeans and my favorite Rolling Stones t-shirt that's just a tad bit snug in the breast area, but I left my hair pulled back. I don't want to give anyone the wrong idea. I'm not here for a hook-up. I'm just here to hang out with my friend while she sings.

And hopefully run into Rider again.

Girl, you are all over the place.

She smiles. "I remember him. He was the wingman. You know that's what they call him on the ice too." Before I can answer she says, "Of course you don't. You don't watch hockey."

"After you left, I asked him if his moves worked on guys, too."

Her jaw drops open in disbelief. "You did?"

"I thought he was funny and I wasn't ready to go home yet, so..."

"So you asked him to hook you up?"

"Yeah, but I was only kidding." I take that moment to think about what he said about my breasts being too big and then burst out laughing. But that laugh is hijacked by a moan when I recall the way he eyed my wet t-shirt. He said my breasts were average, and that's what he liked best. I liked his honesty, liked the heated way he looked at me. His gaze wasn't lecherous, and didn't make my skin crawl. No, in fact, he looked at me like he wanted to worship my body and the hunger in his eyes boosted my confidence. I hadn't had a lot of that after Jason criticized my bedroom moves, or lack thereof.

But wait, I'm not his type, right?

"Are you okay?" Lindsay asks.

"Yeah, I was...he was just so funny."

"And cute too. Did you see that dimple?"

"Yeah, cute too," I say softly, my mind wandering back to that dimple.

She takes a drink of her wine. "So why didn't you two hook up?"

"I don't know." I fiddle with the stem of my glass and nurse my drink. "I'm just not into that kind of thing."

Her hand snakes out and closes over mine. "I get that your last boyfriend was a total jerk, and you're not looking for anything right now," she begins. "But why not have a little fun? We're not talking about a serious relationship, or marriage here, Jules. Just two consenting adults having fun.

Go find out if that man has a third nipple," she teases when the conversation starts getting a little heavy.

That brings a smile to my face, but it's short-lived. "Well one, I'm hardly his type—"

She holds her hands up, palms out. "Wait, how do you know that?" she asks cutting me off.

I give her a look that suggests she's dense. "Really, Lindsay?"

"You're beautiful, Jules. Beautiful. I don't know why you don't believe that. You just downplay yourself."

I snort. "Even if I didn't, I'm still not Candy beautiful."

"Candy beautiful? I have no idea what you're talking about."

"Candy was the puck bunny who interrupted us and straight up asked Rider if he wanted to go to her place, or his."

Lindsay's eyes narrow in on me. "What did he choose?"

"He didn't."

She sits back, her expression smug. "What does that tell you?"

"He doesn't hook up or drink during game week. He told me that."

She opens her mouth, about to go therapist on me, but I stop her. "And two..." I let my voice fall off and bury my face in my hands. Lindsay has been my best friend since kindergarten. We share everything, which means she knows how my ex made me feel after he told me to loosen up. I was mortified, still am. "Jason."

"He was a jerk," she says, pulling my hands away. "An egotistical, self-serving jerk who never deserved you in the first place. You know that."

"Lindsay—"

Lindsay leans forward, her eyes soft and sincere. "It's okay, Jules. You deserve happiness. You, more than anyone I know, deserves to have it all," she says gently, hitting on a deeper issue, one I'd rather not think about. Then again, when do I ever stop thinking about it? I see death all the time. I see people love and lose every day. It takes a toll on me. I can't deny that. I also can't deny that I'm too afraid to put myself out there because I'm too afraid of loving and losing.

Again.

God, Brett was only eighteen. He was my first love. My last love. The reason I went into nursing. I felt so helpless when he got sick, and before I knew it, he was gone from my life forever. I'd given him everything, including my virginity, and when he died, he took a piece of me with him, leaving a big gaping hole in my chest that aches on a daily basis.

"Go have some fun, Jules. Hook up with Rider and forget about real life for a while."

"I'm not sure I can do that, and can we please not ever talk about Jason again?" I say, but there is a part of me that knows he was right. I don't fully commit, in or out of the bedroom, and when things get too serious, I pull back and throw up my guard. Christ, why would any guy want to be with a hot mess of a girl like that?

"Good, because that guy was a jerk."

"Who was a jerk?" a familiar voice asks, and my heart leaps into my throat as I glance up to find Rider and Kane standing over us. My gaze latches onto his, but he's not smiling. No, he's frowning as he steps closer to me and taps his finger on the table. "You need me to take care of someone?" He looks past me and scans the bar. "Someone giving you a hard time?"

"I don't need you to fight my battles," I say and square my shoulders, even though the ridiculously girly part of me loves his knight in shining armor attitude.

"Don't listen to her, she's a lover not a fighter," Lindsay says and my gaze cuts to hers.

"What the hell?" I say.

"So is he," Kane says and jerks his thumb toward Rider. "Unless it's on the ice."

Lindsay pushes a chair out for Kane and he lowers himself. "Great game tonight," she says, changing the subject as she leans toward him, her body language displaying just how much she likes him. Kane takes a strand of her hair between his thumb and finger and begins to tease it, like he's totally into her too.

"Seriously, Jules, is someone bothering you?" Rider asks in a lower voice as he flips the chair around and sits beside me. I angle my body and find it a bit difficult to think when I catch the clean soapy scent of his skin.

"No, we were just talking about my ex. He was an asshole. That's all." Not wanting to talk about Jason, I say, "I caught the end of your game tonight."

His eyes light up. "I thought you didn't like hockey."

I give an exaggerated sigh. "I don't. It just happened to be on the TV when I turned it on." I don't bother telling him I searched every station like an addict in need of a fix.

"Yeah, well, I still don't like nurses." He shifts a bit closer and it takes everything in me to keep my breathing steady.

"At least we're still on the same page," I say.

"And once again, in the same bar." He produces that damn dimple with a smile. "I didn't know you were going to be here tonight."

"Sorry to disappoint." Before he can respond, I ask, "So what brings you here tonight? Back on wingman duties?" I cast a glance at Lindsay and Kane, who are deep into their own conversation. I've never seen her hit it off quite so well with someone before. I really do hope Kane is one of the good guys. Lindsay could use one in her life.

"As a matter of fact, I am," he says.

I nod toward Kane. "I think your brother might have something to say about that."

Rider grips the back of his chair. "Who says I'm here for him?"

Oh, God was he here for me? Did he come because he knew I'd be here tonight?

No wait, he just said he didn't know I'd be here.

"Oh, who are you here for?" I ask, working to sound causal, despite the roaring storm tearing up my stomach.

"You. I owe you a date remember."

For a brief second I think he's talking about the two of us going on a date, but he looks past my shoulders.

"Tall, dark and handsome, right?"

I quickly pull myself together. "That's right, and you don't care what she looks like as long as she has a pulse."

He feigns offense. "I never said that. You really don't think much of me, do you?"

I laugh to lighten things. "Okay, maybe that was uncalled for. So far you've been a perfect gentleman." I scan the bar and spot a cluster of girls near the hall leading to the bathroom.

"Okay, so let's do this," I say.

"Can't wait to see you in action," he responds.

Just then the DJ calls out for a girl named Dani to take the stage, and one of the girls from the group I'd been watching throws her arms up. She's pretty and holds the attention of almost every guy in the room as she sashays up the steps, although I must say, Rider is still looking at me.

"How about her?" I ask and gesture with a nod to the stage. "She has a ponytail," I say and work quickly to dispel the image of me in bed with Rider, him tugging on mine.

Oh boy!

He casts her a fast glance. "She's cute," he says, noncommittal. "What about him?"

I turn to follow his gaze. "He's nice looking."

"Before we do this, I want your number." He takes his phone from his pocket and hands it to me. "Put your contacts in here."

"Why?"

"If I'm going to set you up with someone, I need to know you're safe." I stare at his phone. "Put your number in," he commands in a soft voice.

"You're kind of bossy."

I put my name and number into his phone, and he takes it and calls me. I reach into my purse and pull my phone out. I raise one brow.

"I had to make sure you didn't give me a fake number, and now you have mine. All you have to do is text me a code word, and I'll come get you."

"You take safety seriously."

"I do."

I liked that. A lot.

"Okay so what code word should we use?" I ask.

I wait for him to elaborate and he shrugs. "You choose."

"You've done this before, though, right?"

"No. I've never set a woman up before, and believe me, Jules. I take that responsibility very seriously. If anything ever happened to you..."

My heart does an odd little twist in my chest. Could the guy be any sweeter?

"Okay, code word," I say and think about it. "Wait, you need one too. I've never set a guy up and I wouldn't want to send you home with some crazy organ harvester."

He laughs. "How about..." He glances around the room. "Karaoke?"

"Okay we can both use that," I agree.

"Now what about non-verbal code words?"

"You think we need that?"

"Yeah, say you're over there in the corner making out with a guy and you want out. Give me a gesture and I'll break it up."

I twirl my ponytail around my hand. "That's a good one," he says.

"This?" I ask and tug my ponytail.

He nods. "I like it."

"What about you?" I ask. "The other night when you needed my help with Candy, you patted your leg for me to sit."

"If we're being honest, I could have handled Candy. I just wanted you to sit on my lap." He gives me a cocky smile and I whack him.

"Very funny," I say, my body warming, recalling the way it felt to settle on his lap. He'd slid his hand around my back, generating enough heat inside me to set off the overhead sprinklers.

Hook up with Rider and forget about life for a while.

As Lindsay's words tumble around my brain and entice me, Rider says. "That'll be my cue. I'll tap my leg."

Dani finishes her song on stage, and they call Lindsay. She squeals, jumps up and drags a grumbling Kane up with her. When Dani comes down, I push from my chair and stand in her way.

"Oh, excuse me," she says and is about to go around me until I block her again. Honestly, this isn't like me. I'm completely stepping out of character here, but I can't deny that it's fun. Since I'm so far out of my comfort zone, maybe I should go ahead and sleep with Rider.

"You have a great voice," I tell her, and she beams.

"My friend over there thinks so too." Her gaze slides to Rider, who is now talking to the man he pointed out earlier, and I can't help but wonder what he's saying about me. Something ludicrous, I'm sure.

"He's your...friend?" she asks.

"Just friends."

"You've got to be kidding me? That's Rider Lewis. Seattle Shooter's wingman. How could you keep things platonic with a guy like that?" I hold my hands out, about twelve inches apart, and catch Rider's eye. His mouth drops as he approaches with the guy he's trying to set me up with, and I grin. I turn back to the girl and whisper in her ear. Her eyes go wide, and she turns to Rider, a new appreciation backlight her baby blues.

"Rider, this is—" Before I can get her name out, she sidles closer to Rider, and for some strange reason, I want to call abort, and position myself in between them. Which is insane. I don't want to date Rider and he clearly doesn't want to date me.

Yeah, but you want to sleep with him.

I shut down that inner voice and watch the exchange. "I know who you are," she says. "And I'm Dani, a huge fan."

"Hey Dani," he says in a sexy way that has probably already melted the girl's panties. I resist the urge to look down to see if mine are steaming.

"Jules, this is Tate," he says.

"Hey Jules." The guy is cute enough, but he's no Rider. "Want to grab a drink?"

"Sure," I say, and exchange a smile with Rider before I go off with Tate. We grab drinks from the bar, and head back to his table. As soon as we sit, his gaze drops from my eyes to my snug shirt.

"Rolling Stones, huh? Have you seen them play?"

"No, my sister bought me this for my birthday."

"You and Rider," he begins, a little unsure. "You're just friends?"

"That's all."

He shakes his head, and smiles, like he's completely enamored with the guy. "He's a hell of a hockey player."

"So I hear."

His head rears back. "You mean you don't watch him?"

"I don't love hockey."

"How can you not love hockey?" he asks, and I tip my wine to my lips for a sip. Tate leans forward, braces his elbows on the table, and as the sounds of Kane butchering the song, Jeremiah was Bullfrog, reaches my ears, I resist the urge to cringe. I steal a glance at the stage, and while the man can't sing, he looks like he's having a hell of a time. I guess hockey players are used to the attention. My gaze slowly slides from the stage and searches the room for Rider, but he's nowhere to be found. Wow, that didn't take him long.

I work to ignore the bitter taste in my mouth. I have no right to feel any sort of jealousy. I set him up for God's sake, and he set me up. I focus in on Tate, wanting to make this night work, needing to make this work so I can stop thinking about Rider already, but my eyes glaze over as he continues to talk about hockey. Like. Non. Stop.

I eventually finish the wine in my glass, and toy with my phone in my back pocket.

"And in game seven, the guy they call The Playmaker..."

He continues to talk, but my brain has fogged over. I'm trying not to be rude, I'm really not, but this guy is clearly more interested in the Seattle Shooters—and every single play they made last season—than me.

I pull my phone from my pocket and set it on my lap. I shouldn't bother Rider. Heck, he's probably doing the horizontal mambo by now. Still, I can't sit here for one more second. I'd excuse myself, but every time I try to get a word in, he starts on another story.

Okay, that's it. I can't take one more second of this. I pick up my phone and type in 'karaoke.' My hand hovers over send. Dammit, I can't do this. I can't break up his night. I'll just have to find another way to get out of this situation. I sigh, and I'm about to shove my phone into my pocket when someone bumps me. Before I realize what's happening, my finger hits the send button. Shit. Shit. Shit.

But instantly, my phone pings, and the word karaoke comes flashing on my screen.

Rider!

I glance up, but Tate is too busy talking to notice my excitement. I jump up and he finally stops babbling. "I'm sorry. I have to go." I shake my phone. "My friend needs me."

Tate looks at me like he can't for the life of him understand why I'd want to leave when he has so many more stories to tell me.

"Nice to meet you, Tate. The next time I see Rider, I'll let him know you're a fan."

"Do you think you could get me an autograph?" he asks and I shake my head. The man is far more interested in Rider than me.

"I'll see what I can do."

He flashes me a big smile, and I spin, so ready to be out of this place.

I hurry outside, phone in hand, ready to text Rider when I reach the sidewalk. But when I exit the bar, I run smack dab into a brick wall. A brick wall with big warm hands that are wrapping themselves around my waist.

5

RIDER

Rider

I slide my hand around Jules and tug her to me. Her skin is so warm, her frame so tiny, it brings out the protector in me—not that I think she needs my protection. She's a smart girl who knows how to take care of herself. But everything about her still brings out the defender in me, and while she didn't seem to have a problem going off with Tate, for some reason, it made me go all caveman inside. Yeah, it's true, I wanted to punch Tate in the face and toss her over my shoulder like a damn Neanderthal showing possession.

Dude, you set her up.

"Looks like we were texting each other at the same time," I say, putting my mouth to her ear.

She inches back. "I wasn't going to hit send. Someone bumped my arm."

I inch back to see her pretty face. With her nose scrunched her cute freckles bunch together. "You typed it out, but changed your mind?" I ask.

"Something like that."

I'm not sure what it is I want to hear her say, but ask, "Why?"

"I didn't want to ruin your date with Dani."

"What did you tell her anyway?" I move us away from the door and position our bodies under the shelter of an awning, as rain pounds the sidewalk. "I saw you hold your arms out about this wide...please don't tell me—"

"Oh, no," she exclaims playfully. "Is that why the date went south? You didn't live up to your reputation." She wags her eyebrows and points a finger downward.

I give her a smug grin. "I always live up to my reputation."

She plants her hands on her hips, and I glance at her snug jeans. Jesus, she's sexy in ways she probably doesn't even know. "Then why did the date go south?"

"First tell me what you told her."

"I told her your..." I cock my head and wait for it, but she surprises me and says, "...ego was this big." I laugh at that. "Then I told her you could back it up." She pokes me in the chest. "Now you tell me why it didn't work out."

"She didn't love art."

Jules' eyes practically bulge out of her head. "You're messing with me."

"Nope, tonight I had planned to visit an art exhibit, and she wasn't interested. How can I hook up with a girl who doesn't appreciate art, Jules?"

"Well, you obviously can't," she agrees, and we chuckle. A strand of hair catches in the breeze and slides across her cheek.

I reach out, gather it in my fingers, and move it to the side. As I do, our eyes lock, and her fast intake of breath doesn't go unnoticed. My God, what I'd do to kiss her. But we're friends who just set each other up, which means I can't do that.

"What about Tate?" I ask, my voice an octave lower. "What happened there?"

She rolls her eyes and a tortured sound catches in her

throat. "My God, he was more interested in you than me." I chuckle at that. "All he wanted to do was talk about Rider, Kane, some guy named Luke and another named Jonah, I think."

"You think?"

"I sort of zoned out," she confesses.

"If a guy has you at his table and doesn't give you the attention you deserve, then he doesn't get to have you at his table again," I say, meaning every word of it. A small smile touches her mouth. "What?"

"Do you practice these lines?"

"You think I'm feeding you a line?" I jab my thumb into my chest. "You're talking about the guy who says whatever comes to his mind, remember?"

"I remember." Her pretty brown eyes soften, and her hand touches my cheek. "That was sweet, Rider. Thank you." She's about to pull her hand away, but it lingers, and damned if I don't like the feel of her soft skin against my face. "Wait, what did you say about me?"

"Ah, it's not important," I begin and I'm about to turn when she grabs my arm.

"Oh, no. Spill," she demands and gives me the death glare.

"Fine. I just told him you had a fetish, is all."

"A fetish? What kind of fetish?"

"It's not important."

"Rider," she shrieks, and a few people moving down the sidewalk turn to see what the commotion is all about.

"I told him you were a dominatrix, and I wasn't into being tied up, and that's why we could only ever be friends."

"Rider!" I shriek. "You're horrible."

"Yeah, I know," I say, and she whacks me.

"I am not a dominatrix, not that there's anything wrong with that. It's just not something I'm into."

"Ah, so maybe you'd rather be tied up."

"That's for me to know and you to find out." I arch a brow. "I mean. Never mind, that didn't come out right."

"You want to hit this art exhibit with me or what?" I ask, cutting her some slack.

She sighs. "I guess I don't have anything better to do."

"Wow, you sure know how to make a guy feel important."

She taps my head. "Your ego is big enough."

"...and I can back it up," I say and nudge her in to motion.

She rolls her eyes at me, and she glances up at the sky. "We're going to get wet."

As soon as the words leave her mouth, my thoughts shift, take me in a direction they shouldn't be going. Jules and I are friends. We've established that. Other than Kane's sisters, and my teammates' wives—who continue to try to set me up —I've never been just friends with a girl before and I really like it. I really like her. If we brought sex in to it, it would ruin what we currently have right?

But what if it didn't?

"My Jeep is right over there," I say and point.

She scans the street, her gaze settling on my battleship gray Jeep. "You're not driving Kane's car tonight?"

"No, I had a feeling he'd be leaving with Lindsay."

I grab her hand and we dart across the street, the rain pelting our bodies. I hurry around the vehicle and open her door for her.

"Such a gentleman," she says.

"Marion would kill me if I didn't open the door for you," I say, and then slam my mouth shut, but as I circle the front of the Jeep, I don't miss the way Jules' eyes are on me. I slide into the driver's seat, start the vehicle and turn on the heat.

"Who's Marion?" she asks, and the question isn't unexpected. I opened the door, after all. All she's doing is walking through it.

I check the rearview mirror, and glance over my shoulder.

The rain lightens as I pull into traffic. "She's Kane's mother," I say, my voice even and steady.

"Oh, I see. My mother's name is Grace. My dad is Jack. He's a sports fanatic."

"And yet you don't like hockey."

"Nope, and he couldn't make a fan out of any of his five daughters."

My gaze flies to hers. "You have four sisters. I mean I know you said there were five kids in your family, but all girls." I shake my head. "Your poor father."

"Hey, why do you say it like it's a bad thing?"

"I just mean, with a son, you only have one dick to worry about. With a daughter, you have hundreds, or more."

She stares at me for a moment, and when she finally gets what I'm saying, she laughs out loud. "I never thought of it that way before. Maybe that's why Dad is going gray early."

"I have no doubt."

She goes quiet for a moment, and then in a soft voice asks. "Did Marion raise you?"

"Yeah, sort of," I say. "She was good to me. So was Arthur, Kane's dad. They come to all the games."

She nods and looks through the rain-soaked windshield. "It's nice that they were supportive. My parents were, too. Mom stayed at home. I guess she didn't dare leave five girls alone." She chuckles and adds, "Dad is an engineer."

"How old are your sisters?"

"We range from eighteen to twenty-six. We're all close. When I'm off on Sundays, I cook for the family at my place, or at Mom's, since it's bigger."

"Yeah, I figured."

"Huh?"

"I sensed that about you. Close family, Sunday dinners. Marion tries to do that as well, but it's like herding cats. Kane has two younger sisters. Jaclyn has three kids, and Lucy has two and one on the way. All are five and under, and there's a set of twins."

She gives a low slow whistle. "That's a good size family."

"Yeah it is," I say and offer her a smile.

"Mom and Dad are anxiously awaiting grandkids," she says, and there's a hitch in her voice, like she's choking on the words.

"Yeah?"

"It's all I ever hear about."

"What's stopping you?"

"Um, I'm single, Rider."

I take in her beauty, everything from her freckles to the warmth in her eyes. "For the life of me I can't figure out why."

She snorts and twists her mouth, and beneath the wry look on her face, I get a glimpse of some deeper pain. Her hands intertwine on her lap, and she turns from me. What is it she doesn't want me to know…to see? Not that it's any of my business. While I might be honest, there is a part of me I keep hidden, too.

"Do you want kids, Jules?" I probe.

"I suppose so, yeah. But it's not in my future." I'm about to ask why but she turns the question back to me. "Do you want a big family?" she asks.

"Bachelor for life," I say, a canned response that holds no emotions—one I'd practiced for years. She opens her mouth, and I gesture with a nod. "We're here."

Her eyes narrow as she looks out into the street. "Why are we at Pike's Place Market? There are no art galleries here."

"Come see." I open the door, circle the vehicle and put my arm around her waist. She gives me a quizzical look.

"What are you up to, Rider?" she asks.

"See that alleyway?" She turns and looks into the dark space. "That's where we're going."

"You expect me to go into an alleyway with you, in the middle of the night?"

"Hey, we're friends, right?"

"Yeah, we're friends," she agrees.

"Good, then you can trust me. I won't let anything happen to you. And it's eleven o'clock. Not the middle of the night, unless you go to bed after dinner." She eyes me and I laugh. "Oh, hell you do."

"I'm not a night owl, or a thrill-seeker like you," she announces with a tip of her chin. God, she's so adorable, it takes everything in me not to bend forward and plant my lips on hers.

"You're killing me, Jules," I say and tug on her hand. "Come on."

I lead her into the alleyway, where there are a few people milling about and she tenses.

"Rider," she says, and shuffles a little closer to me.

I call up my flashlight app, and shine it on the wall.

"Oh my God," she says and starts laughing. "That's disgusting. I can't believe you brought me here."

"It's not disgusting. It's bubble gum art." I shake my head and wave my hand toward the colorful display. "Now of all people, I thought you'd see the beauty in it."

She turns to me. "I really don't," she says and purses her lips. "Like...at all."

I hold my phone up. "Look, people have made heart art and fruit art. I think that's a cluster of grapes, and over there, if you really stretch your imagination, you can almost see an elephant in that cluster. It's quite fascinating, if you ask me."

"I think I need to show you my version of art," she says.

"I do remember you saying something about you getting to pick the next place we go."

Her eyes move over my face, and I can almost hear the wheels spinning in her brain. I'm not sure what is going through that pretty head of hers, but she's definitely waging some sort of battle.

"Well…" she begins, her body so close to mine I can practically feel her heart beating. Heat arcs between us, and dammit, I'm pretty damn certain I'm not the only one feeling this. We have a connection, some strange sort of chemistry. And that, my friends, is damn near impossible to ignore.

"Well, what?" I ask, my knuckles brushing up against hers. The second our fingers connect, my dick reacts.

"We could go back to my place and I could show you what I've been working on."

"I'd love to see your art," I say softly, and resist the urge to say that I'd love to see more of her too—without clothes. Truthfully, I want her. I want her in ways I haven't wanted another in…ever. Which means I need to back the fuck off. Only problem is, in my current state of arousal, that signal is not quite reaching my thickening dick—and that guy has a mind of its own.

JULES

I cast a sidelong glance at Rider as he negotiates the damp streets. I honestly can't believe I suggested we go back to my place. My God, it's been so long since a man has graced my condo. My cat is likely to go ballistic, and do I really know this guy? Not really. Yet I feel like we've known each other forever. It's strange, really. We just met, but our easy rapport and chemistry makes it feel like I've known him for a lifetime.

"You okay?" he asks, as if he can feel my eyes drilling in to the side of his head.

"I'm good," I answer quietly, and tear my gaze away to stare out the window.

"Hey," he says, his hand snaking across the seat to cover mine. He gives it a little squeeze. "We can go grab a bite to eat if you've changed your mind. We don't have to go back to your place."

I chuckle at that. "You're always hungry, aren't you?"

He laughs. "Pretty much. I'm a growing boy."

"You're a full-grown man," I say, and take in the scruff on

his chin. Yeah, he's a man all right, and every time I look at him, I remember I'm a woman.

"Burned a lot of calories at the game tonight."

"How about grilled cheese? My specialty," I say, letting him know I'm okay with him coming back to my condo.

"Only my favorite," he says.

"If I would have said pizza?"

"Also, only my favorite."

I laugh and relax into the seat. What is it about this man that puts me at ease? Maybe it's because I know he doesn't expect anything from me, and I don't expect anything from him. Friends, yeah. I like that more and more. My mind turns back to our earlier conversation. He never did tell me if he wanted a family. He sort of hedged by saying he was a bachelor for life, and that tugs at my heart, really. He's a nice guy, super hilarious and fun to be with. Plus, I really like how he watched out for me at the bar, wanting to ensure I was safe with Tate.

He takes the corner to my street, knowing the way since he dropped me off the other night and pulls into the driveway. I glance up and down the sidewalk. It's a young neighborhood, with numerous families, and kids. I bought into the community because the price was right, and it was close to work, not because I thought I'd one day have kids playing in the yard.

But you do want that, Jules?

"You have a nice place," he says, looking at my small condo through the Jeep's window. "I meant to tell you that last time."

"It's home." I let loose a breath. It might be small, but it's all mine.

He nods, but as he stares off into the distance, he looks like his thoughts are a million miles away. "Home is good." He turns to me. "Did you grow up around here?"

"My parents aren't too far. Far enough that they have to call first. I mean I love them, but you know, I wouldn't want them to walk in on me if I was..." Cripes, why can't I stop thinking about sex.

He laughs at that. "You're an adult."

"Yeah, but I'll always be their little girl."

He goes quiet for a long time, so long I think he might have changed his mind about coming in, but then he says, "I like that."

"Where do you live?"

"Out in Madison," he says, almost like he's embarrassed by the rich neighborhood. "Cole bought a home there—he's my buddy on the team, and I found a nice place near him. Kane isn't too far from me either."

"Far enough that he has to call?" I joke.

"Nope, and he has a key to my place. He can come and go any time he likes."

"That's nice that you guys are so close. Are your...uh, Kane's parents nearby?" I ask. He frowns and my stomach knots. Maybe I shouldn't be probing too deeply here. Things clearly went on in his life that he doesn't want to talk about.

"About half an hour away," he says and reaches for the door, shutting the conversation down.

Taking the hint, I open my door and slide from the car. Rider meets me at the front of the Jeep and I fish my keys from my purse as he follows me up the short walkway.

"How long have you lived here?" he asks.

"Just a year. It's close to the hospital." I open the door, and as soon as I do, Peaches lets out a loud meow.

"Whoa," Rider says, the cat giving him a fright.

"Sorry, I should have warned you. Rider, meet Peaches."

"Your cat's name is Peaches." I flick the light on and my tabby lifts her tail and saunters around me.

"Can you think of a better one?" Rider scratches his head,

but Peaches stops in front of him and hisses. "She can be a little bit of a princess at times," I say. "She doesn't love new people, but she'll warm up once she gets used to you."

"Can't wait."

I chuckle at that and turn the lights on as we make our way down the hall. I glance over my shoulder to see Rider checking the place out.

"Drink?" I ask.

"Sure. Cold beer if you have one."

"You bet. I always keep Dad's favorites on hand," I say and open the fridge. I pull out a Dead Man's Brew, and hand it to him. "Double IPA," I say.

"A girl who knows her beer. That's a way to a man's heart you know," he jokes and takes a long pull. "Your father has good taste." He takes another mouthful and I stand there for a second, watching his throat work, but my gaze leaves his face, tracks down his hard body. Eye candy, that's what he is, and could likely charm an angry bear with a toothache. Honestly, Rider is hotter than any man has a right to be, and he's standing here in my kitchen. So, what am I going to do about that? Before I can stop myself, I glance down, examine his crotch. Every nerve in my body comes alive, and it's all I can do to fill my lungs. He clears his throat and my gaze flies to his.

"Ah," I say, my knees threatening to buckle as a tremble quakes through me. "Yeah, I think I'll have wine."

What the hell? Not only was I checking out his package, he caught me in the damn act. Friends don't do that, right? It's a question I can't answer, considering I've never had a guy friend before. I pop open the cork on a bottle of white, pour a generous amount into a glass and take a much-needed drink. I swallow, but it catches in my throat when Rider closes the distance between us. His heat and energy reach out to me and when he says my name, a low growl rumbling in the room, his hot breath tickles the fine hairs on the back of my neck.

"Jules..."

"Yeah?" I practically choke out as the warmth of his breath seeps under my skin and travels all the way to the needy juncture between my legs. My body heats, reminding me I haven't been with a man in a long time. Although, a man like Rider... well, I've never been with anyone like him before.

"You can check me out if you want to," he murmurs.

A strange, garbled sound catches in my throat. How the hell am I supposed to respond to that? "I..." I begin, and stop when his knuckles brush against the back of my neck. His fingers close around my pony tail, and he tugs. "But...but we're just friends," I remind him. Lame, Jules. Really lame. With my brain barely functioning I can't seem to think straight, and if he tugs on my hair again, I might just turn around and tear off his clothes.

"Friends who aren't having any luck in the wingman, or wingwoman, department."

"True," I say, and he comes closer, until his chest is against my back. His heart drums against my body, matching the fast tempo of mine. I shift from one foot to the other, and suck in a fast breath when his erection—his very big erection—rubs against the small of my back. I might not be his usual flavor of the week, but right now, this man wants me as much as I want him.

Go have some fun, Jules.

My nipples tighten in my lacy bra, and my breathing changes as Lindsay's words circle my brain, urging me to give in to my urges. While one part of me begs me to go for it—I haven't had an orgasm without the use of batteries in...ever— the other part of me is a bit apprehensive. Is this too soon? Will it ruin this budding friendship?

I bet he could bring you to orgasm.

"Maybe we could help each other out until we find suitable partners?" he says, his other hand tracing down my neck, lingering on my shoulder.

"What are you suggesting?"

"You and me. Nothing serious. You're not into hook-ups and that's cool, but I just thought maybe for tonight we could be friends with...benefits."

As soon as the words leave his mouth, old fears burst like a damn and my entire body stiffens. Rider's hand instantly stills on my body.

"I'm sorry," he says quickly. "I shouldn't have—"

"Rider," I say, and spin around. Deep gray eyes meet mine, and the desire I see reflected there does the strangest things to me. Before I can help myself, I blurt out, "I'm not very good at this."

He frowns, and angles his head. "Good at what?" I look down, but his rough thumb captures my chin and lifts it until we're eye to eye. "What is it, Jules?"

The genuine concern in his voice gives me the courage to go on. "This..." I say, and wave my hand back and forth between the two of us.

"Being friends?" he asks, his brow furrowed.

"I'm not explaining this right," I say, finding it hard to think with clarity as his heat envelopes me.

"Hey," he says. "It's okay. If you don't want to do this, it's fine. We're still friends. We can eat grilled cheese and watch a movie."

My heart misses a beat. I totally love how sweet and thoughtful he is, and that he's putting zero pressure on me. His words wrap me in a blanket of comfort and safety, and that's something I've not experienced in a very, very long time. Or maybe even ever.

"Jason—"

"Wait, who?" he asks and backs up. I reach for his hand, pull him back to me.

"He's my ex." Rider relaxes, and his body bumps mine as I tug him closer. "He was kind of a jerk."

"Is that who you were talking about at the bar?"

"Yeah. He sort of did a number on me." I give a fast shake of my head. "I have no idea why I'm telling you this." I blink up at him. "Actually, I do." I want him to know he's suggesting sex with a woman who can't let go—can't orgasm.

"I'm listening."

"He...he basically said I was bad at sex."

Rider curses under his breath. "Where does he live?"

Wow, who knew this man would be so territorial, or that I'd love that about him? I laugh, but it comes out rough around the edges, heavily saturated with arousal. "While I appreciate the gesture, I'm over him."

Those astute gray eyes study me. "Actually, I don't think you are."

"No, I am." I blink rapidly and nod in an effort to convince him. "Really. I promise."

"No, Jules. What I mean is you're not over what he said to you. Give me a chance I'll fix it."

"Fix what?"

He slides a hand around my waist and tugs me against him, hard. I might be a strong, independent woman, but this alpha act and how damp it's making my panties doesn't go unnoticed.

"I can guarantee you the problem was his, not yours."

I bite my lip, and shake my head. "No, I don't think so. Look, I just...I have a hard time relaxing and giving up control, you know."

His eyebrow shoots up. "Because of Jason—"

"No," I say flatly and don't elaborate. Jason shattered my confidence in the bedroom, but he wasn't wrong. I do hold back. I don't fully let go. But that stems from my first love—my first loss—Brett. I slam the doors on those memories, not wanting them to invade and break this intimate moment between us.

His eyes move over my face, and I see many questions lingering there. "You don't have to tell me who hurt you, or why you're guarded. It's okay. That's your business. But..." He places his palm on my cheek, his fingers so warm against my skin. "I can build a safe place for you in the bedroom, a place where you can feel free to let go, no judgement, just acceptance, if that's what you want."

My heart pinches in my too-tight chest. Is this man for real? Rider wants to take care of me? The offer is a simple one, but not simple at all. My whole life I've been the one to take care of others, but I'm afraid. After Brett's death, I've been too afraid to let go, too afraid to...live.

"Why?" is all I can seem to ask.

"We're friends, and friends take care of each other." The truth in his words, the warmth they create in my soul, wrap around me and squeeze tight. I stare at the man, and something inside me shifts.

"Rider."

"Yeah," he asks.

I try to look away but he holds my chin and doesn't let me. No, this man, for some reason, is making me stare all my demons in the face. "I've never..."

The crease between his eyebrow deepens. "You never had an orgasm?"

"Well, yeah, I have but just not..."

"Just not with a guy?" I nod and he continues with, "That's going to change tonight."

"Ego much?" I tease, as my pulse pounds in my ears, praying it's true. I tried so hard with my ex, but I always tensed up, unable to just let myself go and enjoy.

"I can back it up," he teases, his words meant to put me at ease, and they do. I laugh, but it dies a sudden death.

"Friends. That's all we can ever be," I state, needing him to know this before we go one step further.

"I know," he says, and his brow knits together as a wave of darkness moves over his face. "It's all I can do too, Jules."

My throat tightens, and I swallow against the pain. This man is damaged. We both are, and now that we both know where the other stands, what to expect, and what not to...

"A safe place, somewhere I can let go. It's what I want," I say, answering his long-ago question as I wrap my arms around his neck. His mouth instantly finds mine, and my lids shut as he kisses me, his tongue sliding in slowly, a gentle introduction, like he's afraid of scaring me off. To show him how much I want this, him, I moan and deepen the kiss. It does something to him, prompts him into action.

"Bedroom," he murmurs, his voice ragged as he breaks the kiss. The black in his eyes bleed into the gray and I'm pretty damn certain no man has ever looked at me with such hunger. It's fascinating...exhilarating.

"Upstairs, second door on the right." He scoops me up and I wrap my arms around him. He rushes, like there are flames licking at his heels, and takes the stairs two at a time. I sort of like his enthusiasm, the urgency about him. His eagerness turns me on even more. The next thing I know, we're in my bedroom and he's kicking the door closed.

A smile plays on his mouth as he glances around, his eyes moving over my flower duvet, and the numerous pictures on my wall. "This room screams Jules."

"You don't know me well enough to say that," I say, and once again think about how we became fast friends. How it seems like I've known him so much longer.

He shrugs. "I know enough."

"Well, I decorated the place myself. Things I slowly

picked up over the years, and I painted the pictures." I slide from his arms and take a step back, examining the room from his perspective. "Do you like it?" I ask and I have no idea why it's so important to me that he does.

"I like it. A lot. Just like I like you." I smile at that, and he draws his bottom lip between his teeth as his gaze leaves my face, slides down my body. He looks at me so long and hard, I begin to grow self-conscious. I tense a bit and he must notice the break in my composure. "You okay?" he asks.

I love that he's checking in with me; his concern means a lot. "I'm just...nervous. You're you, and I'm me."

He takes a step closer to me, his warmth curling my toes as it wraps around me. "What is that supposed to mean?"

"Nothing."

He lightly touches a loose strand of hair, the hard edges of his face softening. "Jules. We're friends. Friends are open and honest, and they share."

"It's just that. I mean I get that I'm different from the other—"

"You're beautiful and I want you in the worst fucking way." The deepness in his voice, the authority and conviction, swallow my words.

I've never felt particularly beautiful before. Most times I downplay myself, happy to blend into the woodwork, but tonight I'm being seen—by the hottest guy on the planet—and it actually feels...empowering. A new streak of warmth and confidence moves through me, and I toy with the hem of my T-shirt.

"When you say things like that..." I smile to let him know what it does to me.

"You like it?"

"Yes."

"Good, because it's the truth. Now tell me again that you want this," he says, his gaze locked on mine.

Consumed with need, I say, "I want this, Rider."

He nods slowly and steps up to me. His hand moves to my face. "You're safe with me, you know that, right?" I nod.

"I know," I says.

"It's hard for you to give yourself over. I understand that, and I damn well plan to treasure every inch of you. I don't take the responsibility lightly."

My chest flares with need. The sweet way he's talking to me, the gentleness in his touch seeps through me, and pushes back my apprehension.

"Tonight, just feel, don't think." He murmurs the soft command into my ear, and taking control, he slides his hands down my arms, leaving goosebumps on my flesh. "I'm going to strip you naked so I can put my mouth and hands all over you. I'm going to make you feel so good, babe. You want that, right?"

"Yes," I hiss and his soft chuckle reverberates through me.

"When I'm touching you, I want you to concentrate on the sensations, and nothing else." He peels my shirt over my head and tosses it away. His nostrils flare and he bites down on his bottom lip again as my nipples poke hard against my lacy bra.

"Please..." I say, and shock myself. I've never begged for anything before, but this man brings out a different side of me, an adventurous side I never knew existed.

"I was wrong you know," he says, as he cups my aching breasts.

A shudder goes through me. Wrong? Has he changed his mind? "What?" I ask.

"I said you were average." One hand slides behind my back and with an expertise I'm not going to examine—not going to care about—he unhooks my bra. "There is nothing average about you." My bra falls and he bends to take one of my nipples into his mouth. He draws it in deep and sucks hard. "You're fucking perfect," he mumbles around a mouthful of nipple.

"My God," I murmur, the sweet sensations going all the way to my core. I wrap my hands around his head, and rake my hands through his hair and hold him to me, never wanting him to stop, until he slides a hand down my body and unhooks my jeans.

Ooh.

The hiss of my zipper curls around me, and I reach for the back of his shirt, tug on it, never in my life so desperate to see a man naked. He chuckles at my urgency, momentarily pulls from my nipple, and in a move that has male written all over it, reaches over his shoulder and tugs his shirt off.

"Oh my," I say, my gaze tripping over all the hard grooves and valleys that define his body. I reach out, explore him with my fingertips, and he quivers under my touch. My gaze flies to his, and when I see the raw hunger in his eyes, it fills me with a strange kind of bravado. I don't want to be a passenger on this ride, I don't want to be afraid anymore. No, I want to touch him, explore his entire body, shamelessly take what I want.

"I love your body," I say and press my mouth to his chest. His soft curses reach my ears and I slide my hands around him and cup his ass. I pull him to me, loving the feel of his hard erection against my stomach. "Although I was looking forward to seeing that third nipple."

"Sorry to disappoint," he grumbles, his voice hoarse, his body quivering as I slide my tongue around his pale nipple.

"Nothing about you can disappoint, Rider," I say honestly, my mouth all over him, tasting the salty tang of his skin. I never quite enjoyed giving oral sex before, but dammit if I can't wait to get him into my mouth.

He grips my hair and tugs, but I refuse to move. I want my mouth everywhere. I sink lower, until I'm on my knees, and pop the button on his pants. I release the zipper, and shove his jeans and shorts out of my way. His cock pops out, catching me on the cheek, and my chuckle turns into a moan when I see pre-cum pooling on the tip of his crown. I lean forward, flatten my tongue and give a long, slow lick. I draw my tongue back into my mouth and savor the flavor.

"Mmm," I whisper.

"Jules, you're killing me." I love that I can turn this hot alpha hockey player into a mess of want and need. He bends, puts his hands under my arms and lifts me. His hands go to my jeans, and he sinks to the floor as he drags them with him.

"You have to know one thing about me," he says, but it's so hard to focus as his hot breath feathers over my flesh.

"What?" I manage to get out as he taps my legs. I lift one at a time so he can remove my clothes, and then widen for him, offering my naked body to him in a bold move I never would have done before. I might be wide open and exposed, but I don't have time to feel self-conscious, not when all I can think about is getting my hands on him, his on me. All thoughts leave my brain as he slides his palm between my legs, going under and higher until he reaches my sex. Deft fingers part my nether lips and I gasp as he spreads me wide. It's a gasp of excitement, not fear.

"In my world, ladies always come first," he states in a voice that strokes my flesh and turns my world inside out.

I try to speak, to say something, but his tongue is on me, circling my clit, and making me delirious with need. Every nerve in my body comes alive, hyperaware of the increasing pleasure.

"Baby, you're so wet. You needed this," he says, and slides a finger into me. My body closes around his thickness, and I quiver as he finds my G-spot.

"Rider," I cry. "Don't...stop, doing that," I breathe out, and lean forward to hold on for the ride.

"You mean this?" he asks and works his finger in and out of me, his tongue sliding languidly over my clit. "Feel good, baby?"

"Yes, it feels incredible," I groan, and he shuffles forward on the floor, forcing me backward until my knees hit the bed. He nudges me until I fall onto the mattress, and he reaches up, runs his thumb over my breasts and gives me a little shove until I'm flat on my back. He readjusts my legs and puts them over his shoulders, and I go up on my elbows to watch.

Oh my God, Rider between my legs, his fingers in me, his mouth all over my pussy has to be the hottest thing I've ever seen.

"You have the prettiest little cunt," he says and my eyes go wide. He sneaks a glance at me, likely to catch my reaction to his dirty mouth, but the spasming of my body gives me away. "You like that, Jules? You like when I tell you how pretty your cunt is?"

"Yes," I garble, and rock toward his mouth.

He chuckles. "So eager and needy."

Drunk on him, I say, "Please."

"What is it you need from me?" he asks and fucks me with one thick finger.

"That," I say shamelessly.

"How about this?" He takes my clit into his mouth, runs it between his teeth and I swear to God I'm no longer on the bed. No, I'm pretty damn sure I'm levitating, lost in the clouds as he takes me higher and higher.

"Rider, holy God."

"I take that as a yes." He nibbles some more, then changes the pace, sliding into me fast, harder, the sharp blade of his tongue lashing against my swollen clit in the most glorious ways. What the hell is this man doing to me? No guy has ever pleasured me like this, turned my body into liquid, but that thought brings on another. I sober quickly, afraid I've gone too far, that I'm on a crash course with no choice but to slip from the tenuous hold on reality, lose all sense of control and fall to the ground without a safety net.

Once again, he reads my body language, and his mouth is right there, next to my ear, as he keeps a finger inside me. "Don't overthink this, Jules. I've got you," he says. "I'm here. I won't let anything happen to you," he whispers. "I promise. I want to make this good for you."

His words, the soft comforting way they're spoken, seep into my skin, climb over the barriers and bring on a calm as they squeeze my heart.

"Think about how good this feels," he says and slides a second finger into me for a beautiful snug fit as he goes back between my legs.

"Yes," I say as pleasure rockets through me.

He sucks my clit, and my hips come off the bed, seeking, searching, my thoughts focused solely on the pleasure this man is giving me.

"Yes," he murmurs. "You taste so fucking good."

I hiss out a breath as sensations center on my core, and the next thing I know, my body is convulsing around his fingers and mouth. I jerk forward, writhe, smash my clit against his face as I take what I want without a care in the damn world. Perfection, and so out of character for me. But this is Rider, not my ex, and we're friends with benefits. I can be myself with him, no judgement, just acceptance.

"Rider," I cry and grip his hair, run my nails through, all the while holding him to me like I'm afraid this is a dream and will end any second. He licks me, lightly pets my sex, and when the spasms stop, he climbs up my body.

"Do you have any idea how sexy it is when you come?"

"No," I say, as heat colors my cheeks. My God, I was squirming and screaming his name like it was my job, like I'd never had good, or rather great, sex in my life. Which I haven't.

"Now that I know how good I can make you feel, I want to make you come again and again. Fuck, the way you taste, move your sweet body, call my name. I fucking love it." I gulp and try to turn away, but he cups my face.

"Hey," he whispers, and brushes his thumb over my cheek, those intense gray eyes of his turning serious. "You never need to be embarrassed with me and I don't want to play games, okay. Let's just be open and honest here."

As he searches my face for truth, his cock indents my leg and I moan. If he wants total honesty... "I want you in my mouth again," I admit, my mouth watering with the thoughts of it. "I like the taste of you, too."

"Jesus." He shakes his head, and an agonized groan crawls out of his throat. I bite my tongue to stop the chuckle from surfacing. But I have to say I love this openness between us. It's...freeing, and not something I've ever really experienced before. "As much as I'd like that too," he continues. "I'm so fucking close, babe, and I want in here," he says and slides a finger into me.

"God, I want that too," I murmur arousal curling around me as my core grips him.

In a hurried move, he grabs his pants from the floor and his sudden absence leaves cold where there was once warmth, but then he's back again, sliding on the condom and repositioning me on the bed like I'm a rag doll. Which pretty much describes the current state of my limbs.

His mouth finds mine and his kisses are warm and sweet as he grips my legs and pushes on them, until my knees are up at my sides and feet are wrapped around his back. I kind of like the way he just moves me around, and arranges me on the bed. Honestly, I like not having to do all the thinking, or all the work.

"You lied to me," he says, and I work to make sense of what he's saying as he offers me his thick crown.

He pushes inside my opening, and I'm so hot and wet, he easily glides in. It feels so good, I lift my body from the bed, but he inches back so I can't take more of what I need. Bastard!

"When did I lie to you?" I ask, squirming and shifting and trying desperately to get more of him inside of me.

He slides a tiny bit more of his thick length into my quivering sex, and I get that he's playing with me. His gaze moves over mine, a slight curl to his lips. He waits to see my reaction and this time I go perfectly still, allowing him to set the pace as he slowly, agonizingly fills me. *Just fuck me already.* But I don't dare move for fear he'll back up again. That's when it occurs to me how easily trainable I am, how well we can read each other. That thought makes me chuckle.

"When you said you weren't after any of my parts," he says. "You lied."

For a second, I can't think but then I remember our first meeting, when he teased that I could be harvesting his parts and I told him I had no interest in any of his organs, namely the one currently pushing open my tight walls and filling me to perfection. My laugh bubbles around us.

"I love it when you laugh," he says, but that laugh morphs into a moan as he powers his hips forward and goes so high and deep it pounds against my cervix, but never have I felt anything so glorious in my entire freaking life.

"Rider." I slide my hands around his neck and he buries his mouth in my neck. Every muscle in my body flutters.

"You feel so good," he says and my hands move to his ass. His tight muscles bunch and relax again with each thrust, and I can no longer think. All I can do is breathe and take pleasure in what he's doing to me.

"You're right. I did lie. I want your cock," I say and I love the growl those honest words produce.

"I think you're a tease," he says, sliding out, only to power forward and seat himself high again. I scratch at his back and struggle for my next breath. His chest rubs against mine as he moves and it stimulates my hard nipples.

His mouth finds mine, and I groan as our tongues tangle. He kisses me long and deep and repositions so he can look between our bodies. "Fuck, I love the way your cunt takes me," he says. I go up on my elbows to watch, and every sensation rocketing through my body settles between my legs.

"I've never watched before," I admit.

"Can you touch yourself for me, babe?" he asks, and at first, I tense. "Put your hands on your clit. Show me how you touch yourself when you're alone."

"Yeah?"

"I want to watch."

"Okay." I can hardly believe I'm sliding my hand down my stomach until I reach my clit, but damn it, I feel sexy. I feel alive under this man's care. When his eyes darken even more, I throw my head back and slide my finger over my sopping wet clit.

"That's so damn hot," he growls as his cock thickens even more inside me. "You've got me right there."

"Yes," I say. His cock rams into me and my headboard bangs against the wall, but I don't care. No, all I care about is the heat, the fire burning through my body, the way his cock is pounding, deep, heavy, blunt strokes against my G-spot and cervix. I rub my clit harder, and an orgasm builds until I explode, a gush of liquid warmth spilling between my legs.

"Motherfucker," he says and pulls back. He slams into me, grips my hair and holds on as he depletes himself high inside me. He stays like that, every muscle in his body taut for a minute, then he collapses on top of me, pinning me to the bed. In the past I might have felt trapped, or even claustro-phobic, but right now, comfort surrounds me. I relax against him, secure.

"What the hell?" I finally manage to say.

His head lifts, and his dimple taunts me as his gaze meets mine. "You good?"

"Good? Ah yeah," I say and he chuckles. "I climaxed twice and that never happens." He blows on his knuckles and buffs them against his chest. "You're such an ass," I say and laugh. How is it I'm so comfortable with this man in such a short amount of time?

"An ass who just gave you two orgasms, you mean."

"Why...why is this so different with you?" I question without thinking.

RIDER

don't know the answer to her question. But I can't deny that I'm wondering the same thing. The fact that she let herself go, trusted me enough to free her body and come all over my fingers and cock... well, that's a gift she's given me, and one I'll always treasure.

I roll to my back, tug off the condom and grab a tissue from the box beside the bed. I set it down to dispose of later and pull her to me as I bask in my post-orgasm bliss. Sleep pulls at me, but I don't want this moment to end. I widen my eyes and suck in a breath to force the oxygen back into my brain. I glance around her room. It's dim, but there is enough light from the moon to cast shadows on the wall and showcase her paintings.

"Homey," I say, and examine the painted picture of a vineyard. Is it someplace she'd visited, someplace special to her?

She jerks up. "Excuse me?"

"What?" I ask at the startled expression on her face, the fire blazing in her dark eyes. Any man who can't see that she was the most beautiful woman in the room, a woman who deserves a guy's undivided attention, is a total douche. But, selfish bastard that I am, I'm glad Tate bored her into my arms, and her bed.

Her big eyes narrow in on me. "Did you just call me homely?"

I laugh—loud and hard—until my damn stomach hurts. Could this girl be any more adorable, and the furthest thing from homely?

"I said...*homey*."

"Oh," she says and laughs. "Sometimes you mumble."

I fix her hair, tucking the loose strands behind her ears. "I do not mumble, and you're beautiful. I already told you that." Why the heck does she have such a hard time believing that? Yeah, I get that her friend likes to take the spotlight, and Jules seems happy for her to do that, and that beneath it all, she's guarded. She said it wasn't because of her ex, and I shouldn't want to know why, but dammit, I can't help but want to know more about her. But it didn't seem like something she wanted to talk about and I'm not going to push.

She snuggles against me, and I'm more comfortable than I ever could have imagined. Normally I don't stay to snuggle, but I'm lethargic, and have no reason to rush home to a big empty house that is the opposite of hers in every way.

"What kind of art do you have on your wall?" she asks.

In my mind's eye I picture the monochrome prints on my wall. "Just the stuff the decorator put there."

"You had a professional decorate it?"

"Yeah," I say, noting the surprise in her voice. "Cole hired a decorator and recommended her to the rest of us. I'm happy with the results," I say. Those meaningless pictures serve the purpose of filling the gray walls and big open rooms. Some are even conversation starters.

"That surprises me, since you seem to like art so much. But I guess I am glad you don't have a bubble gum wall."

"You don't know that. You've not been to my place."

"Please tell me you don't?"

"I don't." I chuckle. "But how it's decorated doesn't really matter. I'm not home a lot, and in the summers, I hang out at my cottage on Wautauga Beach." Once the hockey season is over, we'll all be heading there. I like the cottage, but now that my buddies are filling their houses with wives and kids, it's a constant reminder of what I want but can't have. "The guys' wives all decorated it for me. They insisted on a beachy theme and believe me, there's no telling them no. You'd probably love the place," I say, although I don't bring women there.

"Are you close to the other players' wives?"

"Yeah, we're all close." I guffaw. "Although they've been trying to fix me up for as long as I can remember. But still, you'd like them. Not that you can ever meet them. I don't want them to get the wrong idea."

"No, me neither," she says and while that should bring a measure of relief that she's not looking to insert herself into my life, it somehow comes off feeling like I'd just been cross-checked. My stomach takes that moment to grumble and I'm happy for the distraction.

Jules laughs. "I guess I did promise you grilled cheese sandwiches."

I smooth my hair back, and her eyes follow the motion. "How about I make them?"

Her cute freckles bunch as she crinkles her nose. "You cook?"

"Yup."

"No way."

I press a kiss to her forehead and slide from the covers. I tug on my jeans and hold my hand out to help her up. She slides her tiny palm into mine.

"Why is that so hard to believe?" I ask. Hell, when I was a kid, before child protective services rescued me—although rescued is not a word I'd use, considering some of the homes I'd been sent to weren't much better than my own—and Dad was gone and Mom was off fucking some random guy for money in the back bedroom, I used to make my own food. "I'm not a gourmet chef or anything, but I can get by."

"Okay, Wingman, let's see what you got."

I wag my brows at her. "I think you already did, and I'm pretty sure you like what I got."

She rolls her eyes. "Food and sex."

"And hockey."

"Right, and hockey." She tugs on her T-shirt and pulls a pair of pajama bottoms from her drawer. Now how is it possible that she's making a pair of oversized flannels sexy?

Jesus, I need to get out more often.

"Lead the way," I say and follow her downstairs back to the kitchen. I slow my pace and admire all the artwork on the way. We reach the kitchen, and that's when I notice all the plants under her window sill. A hiss has me turning my attention to her cat, who is lounging in some stacked plush playhouse and eyeing me suspiciously.

"You grow your own herbs?" I ask.

"I do. I like organic," she says.

"I like it in theory, but if it means I can't eat a Whopper Wiener, I'm out."

She chuckles at that. "I've taken courses on their healing powers. I hit the market every weekend. If you're interested, you can come if you'd like."

"I'm away next week." I mimic the action of shooting a puck as she pulls a block of cheese and a tub of butter from the fridge. "Big game against Vancouver. Not that you'd know, since you don't follow hockey," I shoot back.

"Drink?" she asks and holds up a jug of something homemade.

"What is it?"

"Kombucha."

I hold my hands up and back away. "No frigging way, that stuff tastes like ass."

"How do you know what—" She holds her hand up. "Never mind."

I laugh. "How can you drink that poison?"

"I make it, actually. Try it." She produces two glasses and pours the purple concoction into both. "I use organic blueberries. It's pretty good." She hands me the glass. "And good for you."

She takes a big drink and I examine the content. "Yeah, so is a prostate exam and you don't see me lining up for one of those."

She chokes, puts her hand over her nose and grabs the paper towel. "Ow, Rider!"

"What?"

"You can't make me laugh when I have something in my mouth. That came out my nose and it hurts."

"I'm sorry," I say and try to stifle a chuckle.

"If you were sorry, you wouldn't be laughing."

I bite my lip to stop myself from grinning, and tear off a paper towel. "Really, I didn't mean it." I move her hands away and dab at her nose. "All better?"

"Yes."

"Okay, sit and drink your poison."

She mumbles something about it not being poison and hands me a pan as I pull a chair out for her. She lowers herself and I set the pan onto the stove and get to work on the sandwiches.

Jules stands and flicks on the radio, which is sitting on top of her fridge. "Did you rescue that from the twentieth century?" I ask her.

"Like I said, I enjoy restoring old things."

My head jerks back. "I didn't think you meant electronic

things."

She shrugs. "Dad is an engineer. He was always fiddling with things like this. I used to like to help him."

"And yet you became a nurse."

"I did, but I learned a lot from my dad."

"That's nice." A warm bubble fills my chest. "It's nice that you are all close." I cast her a quick glance and don't miss the curiosity in her eyes.

"You... ah...is your father in your life?" she asks. I turn from her. Fast. Every muscle in my body bunching. "I'm sorry," she says quickly. "You don't have to answer that. I was just curious, I guess. It's none of my business."

I don't talk about my past, ever. The only one who knows the shit I've been through is my brother and while I've only just met Jules, for some unknown reason I want to open up to her, and that is just all fucked up. I can't make sense of it. Then again, nothing about us makes sense but perhaps it's the easy understanding between us, the fact that she doesn't want anything from me, and I can just be me. Rider, the guy who'd do anything for those he cared about, not Rider the hockey player who is known for his wild ways.

"I never really knew my dad," I begin as I pull four slices of bread from the bag in the basket. I butter them and add a dollop to the pan.

She stands. "You don't have to—"

"It's okay. We're friends, right?"

"We are." A small palm settles on my back, between my shoulder blades and the heat and warmth that comes with her touch is...everything. She presses her thumb into my muscle and it's only then that I realize I'm tense.

"Dad left when I was young, and Mom. She liked her drink. It prevented her from holding down a full-time job."

"Not easy for a kid," she says and I nod, grateful that she's not apologizing or saying she's sorry. I want her friendship, not her pity. "Pass the spatula?" I ask.

She grabs one from the drawer and hands it over. I wave it in the air. "That's how I learned to cook." She moves beside me and leans against the counter, but her leg is touching mine, like she needs the contact. Or maybe it's because she knows I do.

"And now I'm reaping the rewards," she says and I laugh at that. "Although you were probably too young to use a stove. Then again, you are a thrill-seeker, so maybe you liked the risks that came with doing something dangerous." I grin at that. "By the way, even if you hadn't told me you were a thrill-seeker, I would have figured it out."

"How?" I ask.

She gestures to the pan. "You're melting butter in a hot pan with no shirt on."

I laugh as she teases me, and as tension drains from my body, I say, "Child services removed me from the home when I was around seven. I was pissed off, actually."

"Yeah?"

"We were checked on a few times and I was doing a good job of holding it all together. I used to keep boxes in the cupboards to make it look like we had food."

"Smart," she says. "I like that in a guy."

Man, and I like her.

I toss two slices of bread into the hot pan, add the cheese, and place the other slices on top.

"But the worker caught on when the boxes never changed. Apparently, I wasn't that smart."

"Yeah, you were. She just wasn't about to be outfoxed by a seven-year-old."

"Apparently."

She frowns. "Was it better for you afterward? In the foster homes?"

"Some places were great." I shrug, and rub my hand over my right temple. I fought back when I was eleven, trying to protect my foster sister, who'd got caught sneaking in after curfew. Her old man was an abusive asshole, and I had inserted myself in between them. I was a scrawny pre-teen who couldn't do much, other than give her time to run and lock herself in her room until her father could cool down. The boot he threw at me...yeah, I'd do it again. But after that, I started weight training. "Some weren't."

"Then you found yourself with Kane's family?" she says, injecting a cheery note into her voice.

I nod. I'd gone into the home with a chip on my shoulder, expecting the worst. I take a breath, and try not to think about the first time Marion hugged me. "Yeah, at fourteen."

"I'm guessing you and Kane must have hit it off right away, which is why they kept you."

I flip the sandwiches and laugh. "We were oil and water, babe."

Her mouth drops open. "Really?"

"But we worked it out. I never expected to stay as long as I did." I finish grilling the sandwiches and Jules sets two plates on the counter. I slide the sandwiches onto them, she cuts them in half and carries them to the table.

"How come they kept you so long?" she asks as she takes a bite of the cheesy goodness.

"They discovered I was good at hockey."

She stops chewing, and her eyes narrow. It's easy to tell her mind is racing from the way her eyes are blinking.

"Really?"

"Of course," I say and can't for the life of me understand the skepticism in her eyes. I was good at hockey, I got to stay. It's really just as simple as that. I exhale a slow breath, and honest to God, it felt good to share that with her, but now I want to talk about something else, want to know more about her. I reach for my sandwich and take a big bite. "This is good," I say and wash it down with her poisonous elixir known as kombucha, which isn't half bad, really.

"Really good," she agrees.

"Tell me something about you," I say.

"Not much to tell. This is my home. I like plants and restoring things. Later, I'll take you into the garage."

I go still. "Wait, that's not where you harvest organs is it? Dammit, I knew it."

She laughs out loud as I glance at her fridge.

"What, you think I keep organs in my fridge?" she asks, loving the easy comradery between us, not to mention the smile she always gifts me when I tease her.

"Actually, I was wondering if you had any mustard."

"Eww, you can't be serious."

"Unfortunately, I am."

"Ketchup I can understand, but mustard?"

"Don't diss the mustard." I shake my head. "I'm starting to rethink this friendship, Jules."

"Yeah, me too." She stands and pulls a bottle from the fridge. I take it, pour a generous amount on to my plate and dip my sandwich in before taking another big bite.

"Yuck. That's disgusting."

"Try it." I dip it again, and hold it out for her to taste.

"No thanks."

"Do it," I say.

"Rider—"

"Fine." She reluctantly bites into it, and surprise resisters in her eyes. "Okay, that is good."

"You have a little..." I lean in to her, wipe my finger over the corner of her lip and bring it to my mouth. I slide it in and taste her on my tongue.

"Rider," she says, her voice breathless.

"Yeah?" My dick swells in my pants. Christ, you'd think I'd

be sated after burying myself balls-deep earlier, but no. I want more.

"I like that we're friends with benefits," she says, her lashes blinking rapidly. "But I'm not sure of the rules."

"The rules are whatever we want them to be," I say and stand. A little gasp catches in her throat when I tug her chair back and scoop her up. "And what I want right now is you, back in bed, my mouth between your legs."

8

JULES

Sitting at Nelly's bar, I stare at the big screen along with everyone else in the place, and practically leap from my chair when someone slams Rider into the unforgiving boards. How dare they! I wince and want to look away, but keep my eyes glued to the TV, desperately needing to know if he's okay. My God, hockey is brutal, and in my line of work, I see enough broken bones and blood as it is. Is it any wonder I don't watch? Rider picks himself up, shakes his head and skates back toward center ice. I let loose a breath I've been holding.

"I don't like this game," I say to Lindsay as cheers erupt in the crowd.

She chuckles and arches a brow. "Really? Then why are you on the edge of your seat?"

I give her a look that suggests she's dense. "Because Rider just got hit."

"It's called checked, and yeah, he took a good one there," Lindsay says, toying with the paper straw in her daiquiri.

"At least he's okay." I glance down and fiddle with the

edges of my napkin, needing something to do with my agitated hands.

"Last October, he got knocked out," Lindsay says. "He missed a few games because of a concussion."

My head snaps up. "What?" I ask. That must have been why he was in the hospital. I wonder why he didn't want to tell me it was a concussion. "How long was he laid up?"

She wraps her lips around her straw and glances up at me. "Not long and speaking of laid..."

"What are you getting at?" I say and flick my ponytail over my shoulder. But when I do, the memory of Rider tugging on my hair stirs the needy juncture between my legs. At least the bar is dark and the flush creeping into my cheeks won't give me away.

Lindsay's expression is entirely too knowing when she states, "What I'm getting at is, it's nice to see you finally got some, girl." She snaps her fingers and tosses her hair back.

"What are you talking about?"

"Oh, come on. You're sleeping with him."

"I am not," I blurt out, my first reaction is to go on the defense, even though Lindsay can read me like an open book. Why again is it I'm keeping it a secret? Oh right, it's just a fling with a friend, and I don't want anyone to get the wrong idea.

She snorts. "Oh, yeah, okay, sure," she says and rolls her eyes. "I knew it the second you walked in here. After a whole week, you're still walking funny."

"Ohmigod, Lindsay." My cheeks flare hot and she simply chuckles. But my mind revisits the night he spent in my bed, and how he was gone come morning.

"Rider must have given you one hell of a...ride."

Fine, two can play this game. "Well, you're sleeping with Kane."

"So I was right then?" Her green eyes sparkle. "You're admitting that you got some?"

"Oh crap," I say, and she leans toward me.

"Spill."

"There is nothing to spill." In a move to bide my time, I take a slow sip of my wine.

"I've got all night, Jules," Lindsay says and steals a glance at the screen when hoots and hollers drown out our voices.

When the place settles down, I say, "Fine, it just sort of happened. We were at my place—"

"You went back to your place?"

"Yeah, why?"

Her brows knit together. "It's just that...well, that's out of character." I nod in agreement. Since I've met Rider, I've been doing a lot of different things. "I mean, you didn't even invite Jason to your home until you knew him for months."

"Rider and I are friends." Fast friends, but friends none the less. I toy with the sleek stem of my glass, and shuffle my chair in closer to the table when someone bangs me from behind, hitting me so hard, my wine sloshes over the sides of my glass. "It's different, is all."

Lindsay looks past my shoulders, and frowns, her eyes following whoever knocked me. "Different how?"

I glance around to make sure no one can hear, but everyone is focused on the game. "There are no expectations. He's not looking for anything, I'm not looking for anything, so we decided to become friends with benefits. We're just having fun."

Lindsay sucks in air and leans back. "You think that's a good idea?"

"Yeah. Why? Don't you?" I angle my head. "You're the one who's always encouraging me to get my ass back out there and have some fun. You told me to go for it with Rider."

"I know, and he seems like a nice guy."

"He *is* a nice guy," I agree.

"A one-night stand, and friends with benefits are two different things." Her hand falls over mine. "I just don't want to see you get hurt."

"How can I get hurt?" I square my shoulders, confident in my choices. "I'm a big girl and know what I'm getting into."

A long pause and then, "Do you?"

Wait, does she know something I don't?

Cheers erupt again, and we both turn to the screen in time to see the Shooters win the game.

"Nice," I say under my breath, and clap with the rest of the patrons. I turn back to Lindsay as the team members all hug. Where were we? Oh, right. She was warning me.

"What exactly are you trying to say?"

"You deserve it all, Jules. Love, happiness, the big house full of kids, a guy who'll put you on a pedestal. A guy who will worship the ground you walk on."

Now it's my time to snort. "Who says I want that?"

Green eyes go as serious as a heart attack. "I do."

I open my mouth, about to protest—even though she's not wrong—but my voice catches when I get hit from behind again. I slowly turn and find none other than Candy, with her big blue eyes glaring down at me. Behind her stands her posse, and I hope none of them smile, otherwise the three-inch-thick layer of makeup on their faces could crack like dry cement.

"Candy," I say and shift in my chair.

"You two know each other?" Lindsay asks.

"We met the other night," I say.

"Yeah, when you were pretending to be Rider's fiancée." She rolls her eyes and waves a dismissive hand. "Wishful thinking on your part, I guess."

"Jules?" Lindsay says quietly.

"Are you calling me a liar?" Behind her, two girls share a

whisper, and I arch a brow. I have no time for mean girls. "Do you two have something to say?" Candy waves her hands to quiet them.

"Yes, you're a liar." She pulls her phone from her Gucci bag and waves it. "My girlfriend in Vancouver is about to fuck loverboy after the game."

Blood drains from my face, and a ridiculous lump forms in my throat and threatens to choke me. Honestly, who Rider goes home with—or to put it more crudely, who he fucks—is his business. It shouldn't bother me one little bit.

So, why does it?

"We have an open relationship," I state, my voice even and calm, likely from my emergency room training. Except my damn hand shakes when I give a dismissive wave.

"Oh come on." Candy gives an almost maniacal laugh. "Look at you and look at me. If you had an open relationship, why would he have turned me down last week?"

"Hey," Lindsay begins, but I cut her off.

"Probably because I can give him what you can't."

She stares at me for a moment, her mouth opening and closing, a sound catching in her throat as her friends all glare at me, incredulous. Apparently, no one talks back to Candy. My phone takes that moment to ping and I glance at it. "Now if you'll excuse me, that's my fiancée calling."

I turn my back to Candy and she storms off with her friends. I swallow down the anxiety bubbling into my throat and flip my phone over to see that it's Nancy from the hospital.

"What the hell was that all about?" Lindsay asks.

"That was Candy. According to Rider, she's a puck bunny and well known. She asked Rider out the night you met Kane and he told her I was his fiancée to get rid of her."

She taps her nails on the table. Clickity click. Clickity click. "Interesting."

"Why is that so interesting?" I ask, my insides still as shaky as my hands. I reach for my glass and take a much-needed sip.

"No reason," she says. "Was that him?" She nods toward my phone.

"No, work. My colleague was checking to make sure I can still cover for her tomorrow."

"Don't sound so disappointed."

"A long-ass shift on the Saturday I'm supposed to be off." I push back in my chair. "Hard not to be disappointed."

"Oh, is that the reason you're pouting?"

"Yup, and I should call it a night. I have an early morning. Share an Uber?"

"Sure."

As Lindsay finishes her drink, I pull up the app and order a car. Lindsay is walking distance from my place, so I just give my address. We make our way outside and Lindsay's phone buzzes.

I glance at the star-studded night, and work to quell the disappointment—the jealousy—welling up inside. Rider never said he'd call so I have no reason to be upset and the green-eyed monster belongs nowhere in my range of emotions. We are friends with benefits, and if he wants to go celebrate the team's win with a bunny, so be it. Heck, maybe tomorrow I'll go celebrate with a hospital hound.

Hospital hound.

That makes me laugh.

"Something funny?" Lindsay asks.

"Nope." She glances back at her screen. "Everything okay?"

Her smile is wide and genuine. "Yeah, it's just Kane," she says almost apologetically. "He was just asking if I saw the game."

"Oh, nice." I look up and down the street. "You two are

really hitting it off, huh?"

"I guess so. I mean, it's early."

"So um…" God how do I ask without sounding like I really am into Rider.

"The guys are all going out to celebrate." She frowns, but her astute eyes are observing me carefully. "He said Rider bailed."

"Oh." I turn from her. I guess Candy was right, and he was heading back to his room with a bunny. I really don't care.

Much.

As I struggle to ignore that hot spear of jealousy slicing through my chest, the car pulls up to the curb and I check in with the driver before climbing into the back seat with Lindsay.

"How are your new cups coming along?" I ask, wanting to get the subject on to her pottery and off hockey, off Rider.

Her eyes light and I love that she's found her passion in pottery. I listen intently, or at least I try to as she talks about her new designs. She'd visited Rome last year and it inspired her to do her own designs depicting all the landmarks she fell in love with.

"Has Kane picked out a piece for his mother?"

"He's going to do that when he gets back."

"When is he back?" I ask, not wanting to show too much interest.

"Tomorrow," she says, and smooths her hair back. "So you're not upset that Rider is out with another girl?" she asks.

I give a fast shake of my head. "Of course not."

"Okay, just checking," she says, and we fall silent as the driver takes us home. We arrive and I step to the curb.

"I'd invite you in, but I need to get a good night's sleep for work tomorrow," I say, all the while thinking about that tub of ice cream in my freezer.

"No worries. I'm beat too." She's about to leave, but stops. "When they're back, do you want to go on a double date?"

"Uh, well. Rider and I aren't dating, but we could go out for dinner or something. If he wants to, that is."

"Okay, I'll talk to Kane, and you talk to Rider and let me know. By the way, Kane's birthday is coming up and when we were at Nelly's last week, Rider asked me if I'd help him out with the surprise. He wants to get the guys all together, and I think he's having it at his place."

"That sounds like fun." I say. Nope, not going to feel all silly inside that he didn't ask me to help—or invite me to attend. That would be a mistake. We don't want his friends to get the wrong idea. I wave her off and make my way inside, but the second I enter my condo, memories of last week, the way Rider scooped me up in the kitchen and took me in the bedroom, fill my thoughts.

"Hey Peaches," I say when she sidles up to me, rubbing against my leg. "I missed you too."

I step further into my place, flicking lights on and turning the radio up in the kitchen. As the music blares, it soothes me, and I toss my purse onto the table. My phone pings, and I ignore it for a second, assuming it's Lindsay letting me know she's home safe. She's just around the corner, but we look out for one another, and we have an agreement that we let the other know when we've locked ourselves in for the night.

I refill Peaches' drink bowl, and fish my phone from my purse. When I do, the stupid invisible band around my chest loosens.

Rider: Did you catch tonight's game?

Jules: It happened to be on the TV at Nelly's.

Rider: Sorry you had to suffer through it.

Jules: You okay?

Rider: Yeah why?

Jules: I saw you get hit.

I stare at my phone, watch the three dots for a long time. Whatever he's writing, it must be long. A wave of uneasiness weaves its way through my bones. He was hit rather hard, and Lindsay did say he had a concussion last year. Maybe he's not okay.

Rider: I'm good.

Whatever he was going to say, he must have changed his mind, which leaves me a little unconvinced that he's good.

Jules: You sure?

Rider: Yeah, why? Worried about me?

Jules: I worry about all my friends. You're not feeling dizzy, are you? Headache?

Rider: I don't have a concussion, if that's what you're wondering.

Jules: Just checking.

Rider: Goddamn nurses.

Jules: HAHA. Goddamn hockey players, and you guys did good tonight. Everyone at the bar went crazy.

Rider: Thanks. Can you go on Skype?

Jules: Um, don't you have company?

Rider: What are you talking about?

Okay, I need to word this so I don't come off sounding jealous, or possessive. I don't want a relationship with this man and he doesn't want one with me.

Jules: I thought you guys celebrated after a game.

Rider: I bailed. What are you wearing?

I laugh out loud, and Peaches darts into the other room. Okay, so Candy was straight up lying to me, and I don't want to examine how happy I am about that.

Before I can text back, my phone alerts me that a Skype call is coming in.

A little yelp jumps from my throat and I run to the bathroom to check myself in the mirror. I know what's between us is only sex, but I pinch my cheeks and tidy my hair in my ponytail. *You're beautiful.* As his words rush through my brain, I slide my finger across the screen and as soon as his face comes in to view, my heart beats a little faster. How is it possible that he gets more handsome by the day? I thought this physical attraction to him would eventually wear off, but if anything, I want him more and more.

"Hey," he says sounding a little breathless, his hair a bit damp from a recent shower.

"Where are you?" I ask, and try to see what's behind him.

He looks around and shakes his head. "Another random hotel room."

I head upstairs to get comfortable, but he has a strange expression on his face. In fact, the wingman with the sense of humor seems a bit lonely. Concern niggles in the pit of my stomach.

"You sure you're okay?" I ask as I grip my curtains and tug, closing out the night.

"Yeah."

"How come you didn't go out to celebrate?"

"Didn't feel like it?"

"What's Kane going to do for a wingman?" I tease as I enter my room and plop down onto my bed.

"I guess he's on his own." He bites his lip, like he always does when he's about to say or do something dirty. "Show me what you're wearing."

I shrug. "Just my regular clothes."

"Okay then, show me what's underneath."

A thrill goes through me. "I am *not* doing that."

"Why the hell not? I'll show you mine if you show me yours."

Okay, now that *is* tempting.

"Remember, you touched yourself for me the other

night," he says, his voice growing gruffer. God, I love the huskiness to his tone. It arouses me even more.

"Yes," I answer, my breathless voice giving away the desire building in me. Rider's telltale grin lets me know he's aware of my arousal. Honestly, I've never done anything like this before. It's inappropriate and naughty and I have to say, I like it. I like it a lot.

The sound of a zipper releasing reaches my ears.

"Are you undressing?" I ask, as my pulse jumps in my throat.

"Yeah," he murmurs. "I want you to do the same, but put your phone somewhere so I can watch."

I prop my phone up on my nightstand, and climb to my feet. My God, am I really going to do this? I reach for the hem on my t-shirt, and Rider says, "Slowly."

I laugh at that, and while I'd normally feel silly and vulnerable, everything in the way he's watching me from his hotel room in Vancouver, fills me with confidence and bravado.

I move my hips and he grunts and shifts, getting comfortable on his bed. My T-shirt tickles my skin as I slowly peel it over my head and toss it aside. My bra is black lace, a luxury, and Rider's eyes latch onto my breasts.

"Yeah, I like that," Rider moans. "Keep going?" I slide my thumbs into my jeans, and move them around as I wiggle. "Killing me, Jules." He tugs his shirt off and I take that moment to admire his hard body. My mouth waters and if I try hard enough, I can almost smell his freshly showered skin.

I pop the button on my pants, and slide the zipper down. I wasn't expecting to strip in front of anyone tonight, so I'm not wearing anything special beneath my pants, but when I slide my jeans to my knees, a low moan of appreciation rumbles in his throat.

"You are so sexy."

I tug on the elastic band on my panties, but don't remove

them. He groans at my teasing and I grin. "Your turn," I say. "I want to see." He sets his phone down, and stands. He makes short work of his pants, which were already undone and I admire his black boxers, which hug his package so nicely. This friends with benefits thing is kind of fun. "Keep going."

He tugs his shorts off and his beautiful cock pops free, and while I'm excited, I'm also disappointed that I can't take him into my mouth or hands. I moan, and my nipples pucker against the lace.

"Like what you see?" he asks.

"Yeah, you? I lean toward the phone, wanting his touch, but knowing it won't bring him any closer to me.

"Oh, yeah, but I need to see more."

I reach behind and unhook my bra and before he can ask, I take my breasts into my hands, and rub my thumbs over my nipples. I toss my head back and whimper as my body comes alive.

"Fuck, I want my mouth on you," he says.

"I want that too." I don't think I've ever wanted a man's touch so badly before.

"Take your panties off and show me your sweet cunt," he says and his dirty talk fires me up even more.

"Is this what you want, Rider?" I ask and hook my thumbs into my panties. Ever so slowly I peel them down my legs and toss them aside. I stand back up, and knock my knees together.

"Oh no you don't. Spread. Now."

Heat zings through me. "Is this what you want to see?" I ask, loving this sexy game we're playing. I slowly spread my thighs, giving him a view of my needy sex.

"Are you wet?"

"Yeah," I murmur.

"Open up, show me," he commands in a soft voice as he

takes his cock into his hand and gives a couple hard tugs. Light shimmers on the pre-cum pooling on his slit.

"I wish I could taste you," I say and swallow. He dips into the cum with his finger and uses it for lubricant. "If I had my mouth on you right now, I'd want you to come down my throat."

"Jesus fuck, Jules." His cock jumps in his hand and I grin. "I never knew you were such a tease."

"I'm not teasing. I'm serious."

"Let me see you," he grunts out as he cups his balls.

I reach between my legs, and open my sex lips, exposing my pink wetness to him. My fingers brush my clit and I moan in bliss.

"Your hot little cunt needs my attention."

"Yes," I hiss out, and slide my finger over my engorged nub.

"Since I can't be there, you're going to do it for me." He shuffles and flattens himself on his mattress. "Get on the bed."

I climb onto the bed, and adjust the phone so he can see me. "Put your hands back between your legs, and touch yourself for me, Jules." I do as he says, and his low growl vibrates around me. "Feel good, babe?"

"Yes, but not as good as when you touch me."

"Fuck, if I could, I'd be on a flight home tonight." I love the urgency and anxiousness in his voice. "Tomorrow is too far away."

"Feels like forever," I mutter, and slide a finger into my core. "Oh, god, yes," I say. "I am so wet."

"Look at my cock, babe." I angle my head, study the way his hand is working his cock. It's erotic...sexy. I whimper and squirm, loving the way he's manhandling himself. "I'm going to fill you with this as soon as I see you."

I stare, mesmerized as he strokes himself, and without

conscious thought, I lick my lips in heated anticipation of touching him.

"You like watching?" he asks.

"Yes."

"First time you've seen something like this?" He grunts some more and double fists himself as he lifts slightly from his pillow. His muscles are taut, and his nostrils are flaring as his breathing changes, becomes a little more labored.

"Well, not exactly." Heat warms my cheeks at the admission.

"Not exactly? Care to explain."

"It's my first time in person," I admit, and he snickers at the fact that I've watched porn. But I love the openness and honesty between us.

"Have you always watched, or just recently?" he murmurs.

"When my ex...I wanted to get better."

"You know that was on him."

"Some of it was on me, Rider. I was going through the motions. I *was* rigid."

His eyes narrow, and it's clear he wants to probe, but instead he says, "And now?"

"It's different with you. You helped me let my guard down in the bedroom."

His lips turn up, and his eyes brim with desire. Never in my life have I felt so worshipped. What was it that Lindsay said about a man worshipping me?

"I want to take you to the highest cliff and jump off with you."

"Yes, please..."

"I mean that literally. I want you to experience all the thrills outside the bedroom too." A knot of fear tightens inside me, but in the softest, gentlest voice, he says, "You're safe with me."

"I know," I say. I might be afraid to love, to open my

heart, and to be quite honest, it's a bit shocking at how quickly I'd given him my body, how protected he makes me feel.

"My cock wants inside you. I want your hot juices all over me." My sex muscles quiver, desperate to be filled by him, to feel his every hard ridge sliding in and out of my body. "Can you touch your tits for me?" I keep one hand between my legs and cup my breast with the other. "You are so goddamn perfect."

"Rider," I murmur.

"Yeah, that's it, say my name when you come for me. I fucking love that."

I love everything that we're doing.

"I'm so close," I manage to get out as my brain swirls and my lids drift shut.

"Look at me. I want to see you when you come." I force my eyes open, and they're slow to focus when he says, "I'm right here with you. So goddamn close, too. Christ, all I wanted to do after the game was take a hot shower and whack off as I thought about putting my cock in you, but then Skype... Fuck...." His voice falls off as his hands work faster, and his shameless grunts push me to the edge.

"I want you so much, I might make a mess of your sweet cunt," he growls. "Might mess you up real good next time."

If you're not careful, Jules, he's going to mess up your heart.

I push that thought aside, wanting only to concentrate on his face and words as I tumble over. "Yeah..." I murmur my hips coming off the bed as my orgasm takes shape and grips me hard.

"I might not be able to go slow and easy," he warns in a gruff voice.

"Who says I want that?" I say, deciding here and now, I want to experience everything with this man.

"You want me to take you hard and fast, baby?"

"You took such good care of me, Rider. Maybe I want to do something for you now."

"Yeah? Like what?"

"Maybe I'll wear a short skirt with no panties, and I'll bend over this bed, and let you take what you want."

"Motherfucker," he curses and lets loose a loud grunt. I grin, loving how I get to him. "I'm dead," he adds.

Talking dirty to him, and seeing his heated reactions, pushes me over the edge. My entire body quakes, almost violently, and I work my finger inside myself as my orgasm takes over. I gasp, and come and come some more, my entire body a hot mess, my sex muscles gripping my finger hard as I quiver helplessly on the bed.

"Rider," I call out, and pant as pleasure pulses through me, a deep throbbing wave of relief that drains every bit of tension from my body.

"Yes," he growls and his hand stills as he shoots cum all over his hard stomach. It fills the grooves, and drips down his sides.

"My God," I murmur, my mouth thirsting for a taste of him as my limbs turn to rubber. We both go quiet for a long time, lost in bliss, but our eyes never leave our phones. A comfortable silence arcs between us and his lids briefly fall shut. When they open again, he smiles at me.

"Feel good, babe?"

"Yeah, you?" I ask, my breathing changing to a slow easy rhythm as sleep pulls at me.

"Yeah, but we're both going to feel a whole lot better when I get home and bend you over that bed."

My heart leaps with excitement, eager to do everything with this man except fall for him. Yeah, that's out of the question and not going to happen in a bazillion years. I can't let it because I can't give more than this.

Right?

9

RIDER

I try not to fidget with my ball cap, try not to take it off and put it back on again as I sit beside Kane, who seems in no hurry to put the pedal to the metal and get us the hell home. I might have slept well last night after Skyping with Jules, but this afternoon, I'm in a hurry to see her, get my hands on her—up close and in person this time. Unfortunately, that will have to wait a little while longer. Last night before we ended our call, she mentioned that she was filling in for someone, a long twelve-hour shift. But tonight... oh tonight the things I plan to do with her once I get her in my grasp.

"What's the matter with you?" Kane asks, casting me a sidelong glance as he adjusts the volume on the radio.

"Nothing." I stare out the window, watch the road signs fly by. "Just tired."

"You don't look tired." He lifts his paper cup from the console and takes a drink. I've already downed my coffee, and it's fueling my anxiousness. "You look wired."

"I'm fine."

"Plans for tonight?"

"Not really. Probably just hang out with Jules. Maybe grab a bite to eat." Yeah, I plan to put all kinds of goodness into my mouth tonight. Starting with her gorgeous breasts. My dick comes to life at that thought, and I shift. No need for my brother to see my boner. Nope, no need for that at all.

"Lindsay mentioned something about a double date next weekend." He flicks on his signal and passes Grampa in the big-ass Dodge in front of us. "Did Jules say anything to you?"

"No, and we're not dating. We're just hanging out."

He chuckles. "And fucking. Don't forget the fucking…"

My gaze flies to his. "Your point is?"

"Nothing." He shrugs. "She seems like a nice girl."

"Yeah, she is," I say. Jules is a strong, beautiful, fiercely independent woman who likes it when I take over, giving her the freedom to relax and feel safe in the bedroom. Damn, I like that about her. But I'd be wise not to develop any deeper feelings for her. She told me she wasn't looking for more—and I'm not, either. But it confuses me since she has white picket fence and family written all over her. It does make me wonder, once again, why she's so afraid. Jason wrecked her confidence, but who hurt her heart?

"She knows you're not looking for anything serious?" His eyes move over my face. "Unless you changed your mind on that."

"Yeah, she knows, and no, bachelor for life, dude." I stretch my legs out, and while I might look relaxed, the sandwich I'd eaten on the plane churns in my stomach and threatens to make a second appearance. "You and Lindsay a thing? Getting serious?"

"I like her," he says.

"I hope it works out. That might get Jaclyn off my back for a while," I joke.

Kane laughs and turns his focus back to the road as a Maserati pulls up beside us, clearly wanting to race. But when the guy sees the two of us in Kane's car, his eyes go wide and he backs off. Kane laughs and guns it a bit.

His phone pings, and I glance down to see that it's Lindsay. I toy with my own phone, anxious to message Jules, but she's at work. Why can't I get that woman out of my thoughts?

I rest my head and close my eyes, a strange headache brewing in the base of my skull. Yeah, fucking dipshit Mackenzie Windsor gave me a good body check in last night's game, sending me head-on into the boards, but I shouldn't be feeling woozy this long after the hit. Maybe I'm coming down with something. Maybe that's why my stomach is roiling.

"You sure you're okay? You don't look so good."

"I'm fine." I tug my ball cap lower onto my head, and will the nausea in my gut to go away. By the time I make it home, I'm really not feeling so great. I thank my brother for the ride, and make my way inside my house. After being on the road, the silence is almost deafening. I toss my gear aside, make my way to the bathroom and grab a couple of pills from the medicine cabinet. I toss them back, swallow a mouthful of water, and plunk down on my comfy bed. The next thing I know, my buzzing phone is waking me. I blink my eyes in to focus and turn to see the clock. Fuck, it's past dinner, and I slept for hours. I reach for my phone and grin when I read the text from Jules.

Jules: Make it home okay?

Her concern for me fucks my heart over a bit. I slide my fingers over the phone.

Rider: Went to sleep just waking up now.

Jules: I hope I didn't wake you.

I laugh quietly. She could do anything she wanted to me and I'd still like it.

Rider: Nope. How's your shift going?

Jules: Work has been insane. I haven't stopped for ten hours.

I can't see her expression or read her body language, but exhaustion colors the words in her text. I sit up a little straighter, everything in me going on high alert. With my headache gone, and my stomach grumbling, I text back.

Rider: Did you eat?

Jules: No time.

Rider: I can bring you something.

Jules: That's sweet but I'm okay.

Rider: How about I cook for you? Come to my place after work.

Focusing all my energy on the task at hand, I mentally examine the contents of my fridge. I pretty much cleaned it out before leaving, but I think I still have time to do a grocery run and cook before her shift finishes.

Jules: I can't. I have to go home and feed Peaches. She's been alone all day.

A wave of disappointment zings through my veins, but I'm not a guy to give up easily. No, I fight for what I want, go after it with single-minded focus, and right now, I want to make sure Jules is properly nourished and rested after her long shift.

Rider: The cat who loves me.

Jules: She just doesn't know you. Once she does, she'll see you're loveable.

My heart misses one beat, and then two. Did Jules just call me loveable? I scratch my head, and choke out a laugh. Yeah, maybe I do have a concussion.

Rider: Okay, how about I take care of Peaches for you, and cook at your place.

Three dots appear for the longest time and then her response finally comes in, much shorter than I would have thought, considering the length of time I waited. Perhaps she deleted what she was going to say.

Jules: Are you serious?

I shake my head. This woman is not used to people taking care of her, which makes me want to do it all the more.

Rider: Do you keep a spare key under a planter or anything?

Jules: I don't. But I have one here at work. It's close to my place. If you want to come by, but I don't want to put you out.

At the thought of seeing her sooner rather than later, I throw my legs over the side of the bed.

Rider: But I love putting out for you.

Jules: We're still talking about my key, right?

Rider: Of course. What floor are you on?

Jules: I'm in Emerg today. Just come in through the main doors and ask Sally in admissions to call for me. I'll come right out.

Rider: Be there in a few.

Jules: Okay, have to run. I'm being paged.

I'm about to set my phone down when another text comes in.

Jules: Rider...

Rider: Yeah.

Jules: Thanks.

I smile at that. Fuck, she's so sweet and always so grateful when I do anything for her. I stand, drop my phone onto my nightstand, and with renewed energy, I head to the master suite for a quick shower and change of clothes. Once I'm clean, I shave—wanting to look nice for her— dress in my favorite jeans and navy t-shirt, and head straight to the hospital.

Outside the even sun sits low on the horizon, and I climb into my Jeep and drive to the hospital. With quick strides, I hurry inside and check in with admission. Sally glances up at me, and her eyes bug out of her head.

"Aren't you—"

"Yeah, I'm Rider Lewis."

She waves her hands, her cheeks flushing as she stands. "I'm such a fan."

"Thanks," I say.

"You played great last night. Wait..." Her demeanor quickly changes, her professionalism back in place as her concerned gaze moves over me. "Are you hurt?"

"No. Actually, I'm here to see Jules..." Holy fuck, how do I not know her last name. We're friends. *Friends with benefits.* But, friends just the same, which means I should know more than her first fucking name. What a douche. I really should have found that out, and in an effort to cover my mistake, I lift my hand about five feet from the floor and says, "Little Jules, who's hair is always in a ponytail."

She stares at me for a second and I get it, she's putting two and two together. "Jules Murray?"

"Yes," I say. "We go way back," I fib. It's not true, but it does feel like I've known her for a lifetime.

She picks up the phone, and calls Jules. After she hangs up, she says, "I shouldn't ask this. It's not the time or place, but my husband would lose his mind if I got a picture of us. And my son. Oh my God, don't even get me started with him. Do you mind? I don't want to bother you. I'm sure you get asked that all the time."

"I don't mind at all."

She fishes her phone from her purse, and a few people in the waiting room rise when they see her taking a selfie of us. Before I know it, I'm posing and smiling with numerous people. I don't mind at all. My fans are everything. Hockey is everything.

Jules finally comes through a set of double doors, and the

smile on her face when she spots me seeps under my skin and wraps around my damn heart. My gaze races over her, takes in her blue scrubs. They do nothing to showcase her beautiful body, but she looks amazing just the same.

Don't fall for her, dude.

"Entertaining the waiting room and staff I see," she says, as I finish my last picture and move off to a quiet corner with her.

"I do what I can," I say in a low voice.

I don't miss the whispered words, the hum of excitement as Jules and I lower our voices to talk privately.

She steals a glance around the room, and I don't miss the way Sally is gawking at us. She lets loose an exaggerated sigh. "I think I'm going to have a lot of explaining to do."

My knuckles brush hers, and her fast intake of breath, the way she leans toward me, doesn't go unnoticed. An unconscious invitation? I'm not sure, but fuck, man, I love the way she reacts to me. I resist the urge to grab her ponytail and tug until her sweet mouth is open, welcoming mine. I briefly imagine myself kissing her, drowning out her stress of the day until she's lost in euphoria. Yeah, that's what she needs, my mouth on her, helping her wash away the stain of a hard day.

"What would they do if I kissed you?" I ask, only half joking. I can't seem to focus on anything but her mouth, and those sweet lush lips I want to taste in the worst fucking way.

"Don't do that," she warns, and glances over her shoulder. "My God, I'm going to get grilled as it is, and I don't want anyone getting the wrong idea here."

"Yeah, me neither," I say quickly. A nurse comes into the emergency area and calls a patient. "Wait, I know her," I say and shift so she can't see me.

Jules glances at the nurse. Her eyes are narrowed, her mouth tight when she turns back to me. "Someone you dated?"

"No, I think she was the one who got off on sticking needles in me last time I was in Emerg."

Jules frowns, her expression serious. "When you had the concussion last fall?"

My head jerks back. "How did you know about that?"

"Lindsay follows the game. She mentioned it last night."

The pieces of the puzzle begin to click in to place. "Ah, so that's why you were so worried about me?"

She plants a hand on her hip and juts her chin out. "Friends worry about friends, Rider," she shoots back, but then she covers her mouth to stifle a yawn.

Professional nurse that she is, she presents as strong and steadfast to those all around her, but underneath that bravado, it's clear she's exhausted, and everything inside me responds to the weariness in her body.

"That's right, and that's why I'm here," I say. "You haven't eaten all day, and I intend to fix that."

"Why?" she asks, a teasing edge to her voice. "Am I going to need my energy tonight?"

I get that she's hinting at what she thinks we'll be doing later—what we talked about on Skype—and that she's keeping this thing between us, whatever it is, about sex. A good reminder to me, but deep down, the truth of the matter is, she works hard taking care of others all the time, with no one to take care of her. That doesn't sit well with me at all.

"Yeah," I say.

A grin spreads across her mouth. "Thought so." She produces a key, and reaches for my hand. She presses it into my palm quickly, and folds my fingers around it to hide the glinting silver from observing eyes.

"Peaches might freak out at first, but just fill her bowl with some food, and she'll love you forever. You'll find her plastic container in the pantry."

"Is that all it takes to get a girl to love me?" I tease.

"She's kind of slutty like that," she says, and I laugh.

"So, feeding you isn't going to make you fall for me, is it?" I ask.

What the fuck are you doing, asshole?

"Not in this lifetime," she says with a laugh. She winks and adds, "Don't worry, you're safe to cook for me all you want."

"Good," I respond, and shove the key into my pants with more force than necessary. She eyes me for a moment, her brow furrowed. "You like seafood?" I ask, redirecting.

"Love it," she says, her smile back in place. She brushes a loose strand of hair from her face. "Honestly, Rider, I'm so hungry, I'd be happy with a hot dog."

"I am not feeding my girl a hot dog after a twelve-hour shift," I say without thinking.

My girl.

Fuck me.

Jules is turning as an alarm sounds, and I can only hope the high-pitched sound drowned out the crap I just spewed. The next thing I know, she's waving me away, and running through the double doors, disappearing from my sight. Once she's gone, I head back outside and climb into my vehicle. I head to the grocery store, pick up all the ingredients for tonight's meal, and grab a bottle of white wine. I'm about to head to the cash register when I think of Peaches. Turning around, I walk to the pet aisle and grab her a treat. One way or another, I'll get her to like me.

Twenty minutes later, I let myself into Jules' condo, and a sense of warmth falls over me. Her warm scent of vanilla and citrus fills my senses as I make my way to the kitchen. It's only my second time in her place and it's strange being here without her. Meowing reaches my ears as Peaches comes around the corner, rubbing up against the doorway. Her back arches when our eyes meet, and I set the paper bags on the counter and hold my hands up.

"Hey Peaches," I say. "Take it easy. I've got something for you. I'm just going to reach into the bag real slow and get it."

What the fuck? I'm negotiating with a cat now? I must really like Jules to go through all the effort. I slowly reach into the bag, and she sits at the crinkling sound of the bag of Friskies. "Chicken and liver, all things cats love according to the packaging." I say and shake the bag.

She purrs, and slowly moves toward me. I rip into the bag as she eyes me like she's the superior being in this arrangement, and I'm not about to disagree. "You like these, huh?" She turns, and her tail lifts. "Playing hard to get, are you? Don't worry. I can sell you on them. They don't call me the wingman for nothing."

I walk to her bowl and drop a couple in. They tinkle on the bottom of the metal. She saunters around the table like I didn't just give her the best treat in the world, and I can't help but wonder if all cats are assholes.

"Okay, Princess. You can drop the act and eat. I'm so over this."

Her head lifts like she's done with me too, and I wash my hands in the kitchen sink as she slinks to her bowl and chows down.

I do a fast fist pump. "Point goes to the wingman."

I dry my hands and pull the food from the bag to lay it out on the counter, and the next thing I know, the cat is weaving its way in and out of my legs. She's either looking for affection, or hoping to trip me. I'm pretty sure it's the latter. I open the pantry, but her container of food is nearly empty. I check the shelves for the bag, but come up empty.

"Okay Peaches, where does your mom keep your food?" She walks to the garage door, just off the kitchen, and purrs. "We've really got a rapport going on here, don't we?"

I open the door and Peaches darts into the garage. I follow her and come across a shelving unit with dry goods, cat food and cat litter, but my attention shifts when I spot two freshly painted chairs off to the side. I step up to them, and examine Jules' handiwork. If I had to guess, I'd say they were antiques, and the fresh nails make me think Jules repaired them herself. I steal another glance around the garage and notice a few more pieces in the corner. One, a swivel mirror that's hanging to the side as the stand is broken. Two, there's an old wooden bedframe worn from time. All it needs is a little love and attention to restore it to make it right again. What is it about old broken things that she likes so much?

Clearly impatient with my snooping, Peaches lets out a loud meow, and I turn in time to see her knock a can off the shelf. It dents and rolls across the cement floor. "My God, what is your problem." Her eyes narrow in on me as I place the can back on the shelf, and grab the bag of food. Her lips peel back, like she's unimpressed with me, and flies past me to enter the kitchen first. "Does your mother know how you behave when she's not around?"

Okay, I really need to stop talking to this cat, but then another thought hits. "And don't you dare tell Jules that I was snooping," I warn. "Or no more Friskies for you. Got it?"

She hisses at me and I arch a challenging brow. "Fine, you tell her about the snooping, I'll tell her about the can you tried to destroy."

She gives me a wide-eyed, almost innocent look, but I'm not falling for it. She's evil and I'd be wise to remember that. I fill her bowl, give her a drink of water and wash up again. With the wine in the fridge chilling, I turn my attention to the seafood casserole. I cook up all the seafood, boil the pasta, and make the cheese sauce. Once done, I search for a casserole dish, combine the ingredients, and slide it into the hot oven.

With that done, I snoop around the house a bit more. I head upstairs and glance into the spare room. It's full of old furniture that Jules saved from the dumpster. The sound of a car pulling into the driveway reaches my ears and I take the steps two at a time, meeting Jules at the door. I pull it open and her eyes go wide.

"Did you forget I was here?" I say, and slide my hand around her waist, unable to wait another second to get my mouth on hers.

"No, you just surprised me."

I dip my head, and press my lips to hers. Her weary body leans against me and it makes me want to take care of her all the more. I tug her bag from her shoulder and toss it over mine.

"Come on, you're tired."

"What smells so good?"

Peaches saunters down the hall and she drops to her knees to give her love. "How did you two make out?" she asks and casts me a quick glance.

"We came to an understanding."

She laughs. "OH, you did, did you?"

Peaches purrs, lifts her tail, and saunters by me.

"And what might that be?" Jules asks.

"That she's the superior being and I'm here to do her bidding."

"That pretty much sums up the human-cat relationship." She stands, and her smile is soft. "Thank you for this." She looks around, past my shoulders. "It was such a rough day, and coming home to..." Her words fall off and she swallows.

"Come on," I say, and capture her hand. "Time to wind down."

A garbled sound catches in her throat as we enter the kitchen. "Oh my God, Rider. Time to wind down? It's eight o'clock on a Saturday night. What are we, an old married couple?"

I reach for the dish towel and my brain stalls. Jules and me, an old married couple? Settling in early and spending our nights together. More importantly, waking up together every morning.

That's an insane idea. Totally insane.

And I really shouldn't like it so much.

"You're right," I say. "Do you want to hit the bar after we eat?"

She forces a smile, and her eyes roam my face. "Yeah, great idea," she says, a false high in her voice. I pan the length of her tired body, the smudges under her eyes. Okay, I get it, she's taking one for the team, assuming I want to go on the prowl after a game.

"Or..." I begin. "We can eat, and you can have a glass of wine after I pour you a bubble bath."

"But the bar—"

"Once you're relaxed, I can carry you to your bed and put my mouth between your legs."

She exhales and her eyes briefly slide shut like that's the best idea she's heard all day. "But don't you want—"

I drop to my knees in front of her, grip her chair and tug until her legs are wrapped around my waist. "What I want is my mouth on you. Last night." I grip my hair and tug. "Fuck, man, last night on Skype..."

"It was fun," she whispers. "I've never done anything like that before."

I touch the hem of her scrubs. "Maybe deep inside, you really are a thrill-seeker."

"Maybe you bring that out in me."

"Why's that, Jules?"

Her brown eyes darken. "We're friends. I trust you."

My heart speeds up. Goddammit, I don't take that trust

lightly. It took me years to trust and her guard is high because someone hurt her—someone other than her ex.

I lean in, lightly brush my mouth over hers. "Staying in?"

"Yes, please."

I chuckle.

"Rider."

"Mmm..."

"Thanks for all this."

I stand and my head wobbles a little. Shit. I blink and grasp the tables edge to balance myself.

Jules is instantly on her feet. "Are you okay?" she asks.

I pull myself together. "I'm good."

Her eyes narrow, examine mine. "Rider—"

I shake it off and make light of the situation. "Nurses."

"Hockey players," she counters and we both laugh, but the worry is still there in her eyes. I can't have her worrying about me. I turn from her, and take the casserole from the oven. The scent fills the air.

"We can't have you getting another concussion," she says. "Hockey is your everything."

There is a strange lilt in her voice. And I can't quite tell if she's asking a question, or making a statement.

"It's my everything," I say.

"And you think you're nothing without it."

There's that wavering lilt again. "That's right."

"Rider, I—"

Shit, I don't want to do this tonight. I've told her enough about my childhood as it is. "Have a seat, Jules. Dinner is ready," I say, effectively changing the direction of the conversation. But her words are a reminder that what's between us is just sex. Yeah sure, I'm cooking for her, but that's so I can get my mouth on her later, right?

Yeah, right.

I fill two plates and set them on the table, and then pour

white wine into two glasses. Her smile is appreciative as she glances back at me.

"I'm not used to this," she says as she takes a sip of wine. She moans her approval and my dick twitches at the sexy sound. "I'm usually the one taking care of others."

"Yeah well, how about tonight is all about me stripping you bare and taking care of you," I say, putting the focus back on sex and trying to forget how much this woman is crawling under my skin without even trying.

Her sweet smile fucks me over. "I like that idea," she says seductively.

"Okay, eat so we can get this show on the road." I give her a playful wink and she grins as she forks a scallop into her mouth. The resulting moan wraps around my cock and squeezes. Motherfucker.

"Rider, oh my God, this is so good."

My chest swells. I love putting a smile on this girl's face. "Glad you like it."

She takes a few more bites and sips on her wine as I shovel my food into my mouth. She sits back and laughs.

"What's so funny?" I ask.

She gestures to my near empty plate. "You must be starving."

"I am," I say, my gaze dropping to her mouth. Her lips part in invitation and I let go of my fork. It clatters onto my plate.

She grins, clearly knowing the dirty direction of my thoughts and gives her plate a little nudge.

"I think I'm done."

"Done?" I stand so fast my chair nearly topples. "Oh no, baby. We're just getting started."

JULES

Before I can respond, Rider is right there, lifting me from my seat. He brushes his knuckles over my cheek, his touch soft, tender, and it does strange things to me. My heart pounds a little harder, and my legs threaten to give.

He scoops me up and carries me upstairs. I can only assume he wants to fulfil the fantasy I laid out last night—me in a short skirt, no panties, bending over the bed. But he surprises me when he takes me to the bathroom, sets me on the sink, and drops to the floor in front of my tub.

I pull my hair from my ponytail and let it fall over my shoulders. "What are you doing?"

"Running you a bath."

The walls around my heart fracture, despite my best efforts to keep them strong. "Oh, you were serious about that?" I ask, working to keep my voice steady as his actions warm me from the inside out.

"Why wouldn't I be?"

"I just thought..." I turn my head, glance toward the open door. "What we talked about on Skype. You don't want that?"

His low groan reverberates through me. "Fuck yeah, I want that." I laugh and it eases some of the tension inside me. "But you just worked a long shift." He shrugs. "Besides, we've got the whole night ahead of us, babe, and there are so many things I want to do to you, but first, you need some relaxation time."

God, could this man be any sweeter?

He grabs the vanilla bubble bath and squeezes a generous amount into the water. "Wait here," he says and his footsteps pound on the stairs. He comes back with a glass of wine for me. Okay, he really needs to stop all these sweet gestures, otherwise I'm going to end up falling for him, and that's a really bad idea. Not only am I scared to open my heart to love —I've seen, and experienced so much damn loss—he's made it perfectly clear that he's a bachelor for life. Is this what Lindsay was warning me about, that he's a nice guy, and I might end up getting my heart broken—again?

I struggle to harden myself, an impossible task when he peels my shirt over my head. His gaze is warm and soft as he takes me in. The hairs on my nape tingle under his appreciative gaze.

"You want to talk about your day?" he asks, like we really are an old married couple who share everything at the end of the night.

"No," I say, even though it would be nice to vent. "How was your day?"

"I might as well confess," he says.

I stiffen a bit. "What?"

"Well, eventually Peaches would have told you so I feel like I should come clean." His cute dimple catches my eye as he lifts me from the sink, and drops to his knees to peel my pants off. My panties follow.

My muscles tighten. "What did you do?" I ask.

"I snooped," he says and I relax a little. He puts his hand

on the small of my back, and leads me to the tub. The hot water feels glorious against my tired body. I lean back, and take a deep calming breath.

"Find anything interesting?" I ask.

He makes a face like he'd just eaten a sour lemon. "In the medicine cabinet, there's this strange ointment—"

I splash water up at him. "There is not," I say and laugh.

"Hey, you got me all wet."

"Now we're both wet," I say, and the mood shifts, the air in the room becomes a little thicker, heavier. Lust swirls around us and I shift forward. "There's plenty of space for two."

"You're supposed to be relaxing."

"Maybe I'll relax more with you in here."

"Well you don't have to ask me twice." I laugh as he stands and makes fast work of his clothes. His gorgeous cock is thick as he sheds his pants. The water splashes as he slides in behind me, and tugs my shoulder until my head is on his chest.

"Much better," I say, as he scoops up bubbles and spills them over my shoulders, breasts and stomach. Our relationship might be about sex, but this, whatever it is we're doing here, I have never in my life felt so cherished and safe. It's crazy how comfortable I am with him, how much I missed his touch when he was away. Truthfully, I've missed his presence. In such a short time, he's become a huge part of my life.

"What's going through that pretty head of yours?" he asks.

"What you found when you went snooping," I say.

His chuckle rumbles against my back, and his fingers slide down my arms. "I love all the old furniture you restore. You have many talents."

I bask in the compliment. "Thanks. I find it relaxing."

"It's good to have a hobby. When did you start?"

I think back for a moment. "I was out with my mom, going from garage sale to garage sale. One lady was packing up for the day. She had this gorgeous old rocking chair she was going to toss if it didn't sell." I shake my head, my chest welling up with the memories. "There was just something in me that nearly cried at that thought. Her grandfather had built the chair, and my mind instantly flashed to him sitting in it, telling stories to his kids and grandkids." His hands curl around my stomach, and link together. "It's strange, I know."

"Not strange at all." The rough pad of his thumb sweeps back and forth over my belly, pushing water away like it's a windshield wiper. "In your eyes, it's like the pieces have a life of their own, and you couldn't stand to see that life destroyed."

I sit up a little, and turn to see him. His eyes narrow as they latch onto mine. "I think that's it exactly. I've never quite been able to put it into words before."

"I'm smarter than I look," he teases.

"Here I thought you were just all brawn and no brains."

"You think I'm all brawn?" he asks playfully.

"That ego of yours."

"One I can back up."

"Yes, one you can back up," I say and laugh, but it turns into a yawn. I sink back into the water and lay against his chest. I turn my head, wanting to feel his heart against my cheek. My lids close, and in my sleepy state, his voice sounds like it's coming from a distance.

"You have this innate need to save things, all things. I can't even tell you how much I admire that about you."

My mind swirls, the darkest demons fighting for floor space as slumber pulls at me, compliments of the meal, the wine, the warm bath...the nurturing man caring for me.

"I couldn't save him," I mumble quietly.

Rider's muscles go taut and that's when I realize what I've

said. Adrenaline pumps through me, and I jackknife upright. Water sloshes over the side of the tub. Dammit, I didn't mean to dredge up the past, to bring painful memories to the surface. Not now, not with Rider. Yeah, we're friends, but I can't go there, and he doesn't want to know about my past hurts.

I turn to him, and smile. "So, what was this about us just getting started?"

He stares at me long and hard, his eyes boring into me, and I try not to fidget. "Jules?"

"Yeah," I say, and push myself to my feet to stand before him stark naked.

He scrubs his chin. "Jules, I think—"

"No thinking, Rider. Just feeling, remember?"

He goes still for a second, then his eyes clear and he gives a quick nod. "I remember."

He pushes himself up, and my breath catches as water drips from his beautiful, hard body. His cock is still thick, and unable to help myself, I take him into my hand.

"Fuck, that feels good," he murmurs, but inches back, moving from my reach.

"But I want—"

"You'll get what you want," he says and reaches into my cabinet for a big fluffy towel. He wraps me in it, ties another around his waist and carries me to my bedroom. My bed is neatly made, and he reaches for the bedding and tugs it down.

"Get in," he commands, his voice soft, but firm. My entire body quivers as I slide between my soft sheets, excited to have the smell of him in my bed come morning. But I don't want to think about morning, or how I know he'll sneak away before sunrise. Although it's for the best. I have my family coming for dinner, and he shouldn't be here.

I flatten myself and he crawls onto the bed. His eyes never leave mine as he runs his fingers over my arms.

"Hands above your head," he whispers.

"What?" I frown at him.

"I want to do things to you."

"I...want that too."

"Then hands above your head." He gestures with a nod to the headboard. "Hold the slats and don't move them."

"Rider—"

"Yes." His eyes are dark and serious but also brimming with need...for me.

"What are you...doing?"

"I'm creating a safe place for you. I want your hands up and your eyes closed. Like you said, this isn't about thinking." He slants his head. "You trust me to take care of you?"

"I do," I say, "But I want to touch you too."

A warm smile curls up his lips. He likes the idea of me touching him too. "You will, but right now, this is all about you."

My throat squeezes tight, and Lindsay's warning bursts to the forefront of my brain. Am I giving too much of myself here? Will this end in emotional suicide for me? Rider must sense the change in me.

"Hey, we don't have to do anything you don't want to do."

"I want to, do it all," I say quickly, to reassure him, even though I'm not certain it's a good idea myself.

"Are you scared?"

"Giving up all control is difficult for me."

Stop being a chickenshit, Jules.

"With great risk comes great reward," he murmurs.

"Quoting Thomas Jefferson, now are you?"

His soft laugh falls over me, the warmth of his breath raising the hairs on my arms. "Actually, I'm quoting Coach."

I chuckle slightly, and it turns to a soft moan when his hands brush my hair from my face, his thumb tracing my nose and mouth.

"You are so beautiful," he murmurs. "Now trust me and close your eyes. I promise to take good care of you."

I pinch my eyes shut tightly, even though I'd love to open them, see the heat in his eyes as he looks at me. But as darkness surrounds me, a little thrill goes through me. I can't deny there is something exciting about letting myself go and living in the moment. Honestly, being in control all the time, being afraid of everything is exhausting.

"You're beautiful too," I say and his mouth closes over mine. His kiss is soft at first, but when I lift my hips, rub my sex against his raging erection, his tongue finds mine.

"Keep that up, and I'll ruin you," he says and shifts his body. He slides a hand between my legs, and slides a thick finger into me.

"Yesss," I hiss and rock against his finger. His palm presses against my clit, and a keening cry escapes my throat. He swallows it with his kisses, and moves his mouth to my ear.

"I wasn't kidding last night. I want you so fucking much, I'm going to make a mess of your sweet cunt." I'm so turned on, my muscles quiver, my climax building. "Oh, yeah, you like that idea, do you?"

Since his finger is inside me, feeling my body's reaction, there is no hiding my arousal.

"Please, make a mess of me," I say, and ignore those knowing little bells jangling in the back of my brain—this man could very well ruin me in so many ways.

"You want my fat cock in you, baby?"

"It's all I've been able to think about since you've been gone," I admit, and he goes lower on the bed, takes my clit into his mouth. "Oh, that's it," I cry out.

He nibbles on me. "I nearly lost my mind watching you touch yourself last night."

"You liked that?"

"Yes."

"I'd do it again," I tease, "But I was ordered to keep my hands above my head."

"That's right, I'm in charge of your body and your orgasms tonight, babe. You don't have to do a goddamn thing but lay back and enjoy."

"Rider," I say as I exhale. "But I—"

"Shh," he says, quieting my protest. I want to get my hands and mouth on him, but following his rules, and letting him take charge comes with its own excitement. After always being the one responsible, taking care of everyone else, I could get used to this kind of treatment.

Careful, Jules.

All good things come to an end.

I let my head fall back and his mouth finds my nipples. His tongue swirls over my aching buds, and he bites down, only to lick them to ease the sting left behind. Sensations shoot through me, settle between my legs, and I whimper.

"That's it. Make noise for me. Show me how much you like this," he says.

I turn my head from side to side as he presses wet, open-mouthed kisses to my stomach, going lower until he finds my sex.

"Has your pretty little cunt been missing me?"

"So much," I say, and move my hips.

He chuckles. "Need something, Jules?"

"Your mouth, please," I say, and shock myself. This man definitely brings out another side to me.

"That's a girl. Don't ever hold back with me. Anything you want, I'll give you."

My heart lurches.

Don't go there, Jules. Don't think about what you might want. You can't take that pain of loss.

He slides a second finger into my body, circles my

engorged clit with his tongue, and whispers dirty words. The trifecta pushes me over the edge and I give into the pleasure pulling at me.

"Oh, Rider," I cry out, and buck against his face, a shameless move that I'm not one bit ashamed of.

"Yeah, come all over my mouth, babe."

I come and come and come some more, until my lethargic body is nothing but a limp doll on the bed. I try to move my arms, to pull him to me, but I can't seem to make them work.

"Rider," I say. "I want to touch you."

"Keep your eyes closed. Relax, okay. I'll be right back."

I close my eyes, and sleep pulls at me in my post-orgasmic state. But I can't go to sleep. I want to take care of Rider. I want to feel him inside me. The sound of water rushing in the bathroom reaches my ears, and his footsteps are soon back on my bedroom floor.

"I'm going to wash you up," he says quietly.

I exhale a contented moan, and whimper slightly when he places a warm cloth between my legs.

"Oh, that's so nice."

His touch is soft, so achingly gentle, it seeps into my bloodstream and drags me under. I try to open my eyes, but they are too heavy, my body too weak.

"Rider," I say again.

"Shh," he whispers as the mattress dips beside me, and the next thing I know, he's spooning me from behind, his warm hard body pressed against mine, taking me deeper and deeper into a place where nothing exists but this man.

Many hours later, I peel my eyes open, and nearly jump from my bed when a warm body shifts beside me. Memories from last night infiltrate my sleepy brain, and I roll to my side. The second I look at the man stretched out, his bronzed body hard and beautiful, my need for him catches me off guard. My God, he did the most beautiful things for me, and to me, last night, and instead of reciprocating, I fell asleep in his strong, protective arms.

Guilt eats at me, but it's short-lived, because as I take in this sleeping man, I understand last night played out the way he wanted it too. He wanted to take care of me, and got as much enjoyment out of it as I did.

Well, that's fine. But this morning is all about him, and no way am I going to spend one moment examining how happy I am that he hadn't snuck out under the cover of darkness.

But I might spend two.

RIDER

I moan as my cock thickens, a warm mouth doing the most delicious things to my body. I shift in the bed, half asleep, and move against my pillow. I grip the headboard slats, and groan. Fuck, I must be dreaming. If I am, I sure as hell don't want to wake up. Not when I feel this good.

The soft moan from between my legs pulls me wider awake, and I blink my eyes open. I lift my head and my heart jumps at the gorgeous sight of Jules nestled between my legs, her lush lips around my cock.

"Jesus," I say and Jules glances up at me, her long hair falling over her shoulders as she worships my cock. "Jules..." My voice is hoarse and breathless, but it's not from sleep.

"Good morning," she says.

"Yeah." Christ, she's reduced me to one-word responses.

"I figured since you put me to sleep like this, it's only fair I wake you up the same way."

"I like the way you think," I murmur, and grab a fistful of her hair. I tug until her lips part, and she dips her head and takes me to the back of her throat. "That feels so good, babe."

"Mmm," she moans, one hand fisting me as the other goes to my balls. She rubs softly, gently, and works both her mouth and hand over my hard length. Man, how I'd love to wake up like this every morning—with her. But I don't do sleepovers.

You just did, dude.

But I can't think about that right now. Not when Jules is working my cock like it's her goddamn job. "You are so good at that."

My encouraging words do something to her, and she takes me deeper, until she's choking a bit. I grip her hair and try to pull her back, but she won't have any of that.

"Oh my fuck," I say and hold on for the ride.

My body tightens, every sensation centered between my legs as she licks the pre-cum from my crown and moans like it's the best thing she's ever tasted.

"You're killing me, baby," I moan, and her soft chuckle reverberates straight to my balls and brings on an orgasm. I tug on her hair to move her off me, but she shakes me off. Oh man, is this really happening? I never come down a woman's throat, but goddammit, I want to fill this woman with my cum. I want in her body, everywhere. I want a part of me in her when I leave her place today, and that is totally fucked up.

Unable to hold it back, I spurt my seed into her, and she gulps and swallows and tries to drink me all in, but I'm coming so hard I spill out of her. My body spasms, and convulses and I lift from the pillow to see her pretty face as she laps at me. I finally stop coming, and this time I'm able to tug her off me. She keeps her hands on my balls, a soft, soothing massage as I wipe her mouth clean.

"You're incredible, Jules." She smiles at me. "You didn't have to do that."

"I wanted to," she says.

"But ladies first," I say and tug her to me.

"Today we're playing by my rules," she says and settles on

my chest, yawning. My heart pounds hard against her cheek as I try to come back from that mind-blowing climax. I brush her hair from her face, ready to put my mouth between her legs, but she sighs softly and closes her eyes. "Still tired?" I ask.

"I am."

"We were up late."

"Yeah," she says softly, dreamily, like she's remembering all the things I did to put her to sleep.

"Do you want to sleep?"

"For a little bit," she murmurs.

"Okay, you rest, and I'll make us something to eat."

"You don't have to do that," she says quietly. "I can cook after a quick nap."

"It's okay. I'm awake. I can't stay long anyway. I have practice this afternoon."

"Oh, okay," she says quietly, a hint of disappointment in her voice. I lean down and place a soft kiss onto her forehead, and she smiles up at me. It produces a tightening in my chest, right around the vicinity of my heart.

"Sleep," I whisper, and she rolls to the side. I stay put, until I hear her soft breathing sounds. Once she's asleep, I quietly climb from the bed, and make my way to the bathroom. I splash water onto my face, and snatch my clothes off the floor. I dress and Peaches curls around my legs when I exit the bathroom.

"Oh, nice to me now, are you?" I whisper. "Only because you're looking for food."

She curls around my legs, and I grip the rail before I tumble down the stairs. Maybe that's her plan after all. "Just so you know. I outed myself to Jules. You no longer have anything over my head." Christ, when did I start talking to cats? I follow her and she's all sweet peaches until I fill her bowl. No longer needing me, she offers her tail and saunters away. "Yeah, that's what I thought," I say.

I spend the next few minutes making coffee and whipping up some eggs. I swallow half the brew in my cup, giving Jules time to rest, and as the caffeine works its way through my body, I feel much more alive. I have practice this afternoon, which means I should have been in my own bed, getting a good night's sleep. But no, I couldn't keep my hands off Jules. The woman is an addiction I can't quite quit.

I take her plate of eggs, and coffee and head upstairs, but she's still fast asleep when I enter her room. I gaze at her for a moment, all warm soft and adorable twisted in the sheets. I don't have the heart to wake her, so I fix the bedding around her, and leave her to sleep the day away. As hard as it is to walk away, I make my way back downstairs put the scrambled eggs in the fridge, and pull my cell from my pocket and send Jules a text.

Rider: Eggs are in the fridge. You were sound asleep and I didn't want to wake you. I'll catch up with you later.

I hit send, tuck my phone back in, and with the key she'd given me last night, head outside and lock up behind myself. The laughter of kids playing at a nearby park reach my ears and my stomach knots. Jules moved into an up-and-coming neighborhood with young families. No matter what she says, she wants this. She wants the white picket fence, the kids, and all the animals.

So, what's holding her back? I revisit last night's conversation.

I couldn't save him.

I don't have to be Einstein to understand someone very important in her life, someone she loved dearly, had died, and it left her feeling helpless, and vulnerable—a big gaping hole in her heart. But life is fucking short, and she can't remain in hiding forever. She needs to experience more instead of just going through the motions. She needs to feel the thrill of living again. I'm not sure why that's so important to me, I only know that it is. But with her, baby steps are required, so baby steps is what I'll give her.

I stop at home, shower quickly and grab my gear. An hour later, I'm at the rink and the guys are all pouring in. We have an out of town game Wednesday and I need to get my mind on that, and off Jules. I also need to finalize Kane's birthday party Saturday night. I tighten the laces on my skates and glide out to Kane as he takes a shot on the net.

"Hey," he says, his gaze moves over my face. "You don't seem as keyed up as you were yesterday."

"Got a good night's sleep," I say, and steal the puck from him after the goaltender Alek, aka the Puck Charmer, shoots it back to us.

"Oh, is that what you got last night," he teases.

I check him with my shoulder. "What's that supposed to mean?"

"I spent the night with Lindsay. Jules is her best friend, remember?"

"Yeah, I remember."

"Girls talk, bro."

We slap our sticks on the ice and fight for the puck. "Yeah, so I went to her place. What's the big deal?"

"Nothing. Glad to see you getting out." He steals the puck and shoots it. It pings off the net and I go after it, but Kane is faster, getting to it first. "You two getting serious?"

"No," I say quickly.

"Good, because Alek," he says, nodding to the net, "saw us out at karaoke. He was wondering who she was."

Anger bubbles up inside of me. But Kane is watching me closely, so I tamp it down. "Oh yeah. She's not his normal type." I laugh, but it's edgy. "He's called the Puck Charmer for a reason, and it's not because he stops all the biscuits from going in the net." Alek might be the biggest player on the team, but I like him, I really do, but goddammit, now I want to wrap my hands around his neck and squeeze.

"Yeah, he likes the bunnies, but—"

"But nothing. I'm not letting a guy like that around Jules."

"So you like her then?"

Fuck.

"Of course I like her. We're friends, and I'm not about to let her get mixed up with a guy who only wants her for sex."

"Um, how is that any different than the relationship you have with her?"

"We're friends, Kane. I just said that. Do I need to talk slower, use smaller words?" I shoot back, ribbons of anger wrapping around my chest and suffocating me.

Kane throws his hands up, and skates back a few inches. "Whoa, bro. Just a question."

"I'm sorry," I say. Shit, why am I acting like a possessive prick? This is my bro, and doesn't deserve shit from me. "I think maybe I didn't get enough sleep last night."

"It's okay. Come on. Let's go practice."

I follow him to center ice, my thoughts racing. Honestly, if Jules wants to go out with Alek, who am I to stop her? I can't give her more, not that she's asking, and while Alek might be a player, lots of guys on the team were before they met the right woman. Jules is definitely the kind of nice girl any guy would change for. Who knows, maybe the two will find true love. I mean, I want that for her. I wouldn't want to come between her and happiness. If that means standing back while she dates Alek, well then...

Fuck me.

We spend the next couple hours doing drills, and I'm not sure why, or maybe I am, but every chance I get to shoot the puck at Alek—harder than necessary in a practice—I take it. Soon enough he's looking at me like he can't understand what the fuck is wrong with me.

Once practice is over, we make our way to the locker room and Coach follows us in. He's casting me curious glances, but I avoid him. I change, and head out before he can call me on my shit. We have a game in three days and I need to get my shit together.

As I drive home, my cell rings and I hate how much I hope it's Jules. I check the phone, and it's Jaclyn, asking if I can stop over and watch the kids for an hour while she goes to yoga. Since Caleb isn't home yet, and Lord knows the woman can use a break, I turn my vehicle around. Odd though, she usually calls Kane first. Then again, maybe he's hooking up with Lindsay this afternoon. Which reminds me, I need to call her and give her directions to my place so she can bring Kane there Saturday night for his surprise party.

Shit, earlier Kane said the two women talk, hell they're best friends, so they likely share everything, which means Jules would know about the surprise party. I should invite her because we're friends, but what would the guys think? I never take a woman to any of the parties or events. I actually usually pick them up there if I'm looking for a hook-up. Would Jules want an invitation, or not? I mean, she doesn't want anyone to get the wrong idea any more than I do. She straight up told me that.

I drive along Jaclyn's street slowly. Numerous kids are running around like they're hyped up on energy drinks.

Mothers chase their kids as fathers kick back in their lawn chairs and tend to the ones running through the sprinklers on this unusually hot spring day.

I creep down the road and pull into Jaclyn's driveway. She's already at the door waiting for me, and gives me a grateful hug when I enter.

"Thank you," she says. "The kids are all lotioned and they're excited to go to the park."

"Go," I say and give her a nudge.

"Are you sure you're okay taking care of them alone?"

"Yeah, I'm fine. I think."

"I would have called Mom and Dad, but Kane…"

She lets her voice fall off.

"What about Kane?"

"Oh," she shrugs and fusses with something in her purse, like she can't bring herself to look at me. "He just said you weren't doing anything today, and probably wouldn't mind."

"How thoughtful of him, and I don't mind." I like her rug rats, but she's never left me alone with them before. Not that she doesn't trust me. She just knows when it comes to kids, I'm a little out of my element. Then again, am I? How many homes have I been in where I had to step in and be the big brother, take on the protective role?

"Uncle Rider," Cameron says as he comes barreling down the hall, Carly and Carter right on his heel. The twins jump onto my feet for a ride and Cameron is talking nonstop about Fortnight.

"You sure you got this?" Jaclyn asks, her nose crinkled.

"Yeah, I got it."

"There are phone numbers on the fridge if you need help, and snacks in the bag for the park. I'll only be an hour."

"If I need any help, I know who to call."

"Oh, who is that?" she asks with a hand on her hip.

"Just a friend, who is good with kids."

"Care to elaborate?"

"No, now go before you're late." I practically push her out the door, and three excited children bounce around me. "Okay, who wants to go to the park?" A chorus erupts around me and I scoop up Carter as he holds his hands up to me. Carly wants up too, so I put her on my other hip. "Cameron, can you grab the bag."

We step outside and we wave Jaclyn off as I lock up and make my way down the sidewalk. We get greeted at nearly every house and I can't help but think this neighborhood isn't much different from Jules'. We cross the street, take the corner, and run into a yard sale. My eye instantly goes to the old round table with claw feet. The piece is old and tired, but with the right touch it could be magnificent.

I set Carly and Carter down and get all three to hold hands while I step up to the owner of the house. The little ones grumble with the delay, but no way can I walk away from such a treasure. Jules would love it and I want to put a smile on her face more than anything.

"How much for the table?"

The elderly lady with silver hair smiles at me. "Those are Jaclyn's little ones."

"Yeah, I'm their Uncle Rider," I say, even though technically I'm not their uncle. Dammit, I really want to be, though.

"I know who you are," she says. "I'm a big fan."

"Thank you."

"For you, that piece is two hundred dollars."

The kids grumble some more and tug on me. The lady laughs and I whip out my wallet. "Can you hold it for me? I'll pick it up in about an hour."

"It's yours."

"I really appreciate it."

"Good luck on Wednesday's game."

I eventually get the kids to the park, and Cameron heads to the slides as Carly and Carter go to the swings. I push them and keep one eye on Cameron. My God, I have no idea how Jaclyn does it. After a few minutes with the three, I'm ready for a nap.

The hour goes by pretty fast and we make our way back home to find Jaclyn pulling into the driveway. She looks far more relaxed now than she did earlier. Her face lights up when she sees us and I'm sure I spot a hint of relief in her eyes.

"How were they?"

"Excellent," I say, and bend to give them all a hug.

"I really appreciate it, Rider. You're a good uncle."

"Well, I'm not really—"

"Hey," she says and whacks me.

"Why are you always hitting me?"

"Because I don't want to hear that kind of talk. You're family. End of discussion."

My heart warms. Yeah, they've all been my family since I was fourteen, and while I love them all, and appreciate them, there is a part of me that still feels the chasm. It might take having my own family for me to feel whole.

But I'm a nothing, a nobody, and any girl deserves better right? I mean, people only love me because I'm a hockey player, right?

Jules doesn't even like hockey players.

Does that mean she likes me for who I am?

What the hell am I saying? We're friends. Friends with benefits, but still. Just friends.

"You want to stay for dinner?" Jaclyn asks. "I made a ton of food."

While that sounds like a great idea, I say, "No, I have to go, but thanks anyway."

She goes up on her toes and gives me a hug. "Thanks for babysitting, and bring her by sometime."

"Bring who by?"

"Whoever you bought that antique table for."

My head rears back. "What the..." I bite back the curse since the kids are within earshot.

Jaclyn's laugh fills the air. "You're in the 'burbs, bro. Rumor spreads fast around these parts."

I grumble curses under my breath and head back to pick up Jules' table. I load it into my Jeep, tie it down as best as I can, and head straight to Jules' place. I can't fucking wait to see the look on her face when she sees this beauty. I bet I can even guess where she'll put it.

I reach her place, park behind her car in the driveway and grab the table from the back. Without even noticing the neighbors or anything going on around me, I head to her front door. I have a key, but I'm not about to use it. Instead I knock, and my face falls when a man opens the door.

"Oh, hi," I say, completely thrown off to find some guy answering. The man stands there, gawking at me, and I feel like a goddamn idiot for showing up at her place unannounced. "Um, is Jules home?" I glance over my shoulder and see the cars lining the road. What the hell is going on?

"Jules," the man calls out, still staring at me with wide-eyed recognition. Jules comes rushing around the corner, her ponytail bouncing, and the gentleman pulls her into his arms. A rush of jealousy I have no right to feel zings through me. "You have some explaining to do, dear daughter."

I relax. This is her father. Oh, shit. This is her father, and it's Sunday. I walked straight into a family dinner. I stand a little straighter.

"I should go," I say quickly and spin.

"Wait," Jules says, and I turn back around. "What do you have?" Her eyes narrow in on the table.

"I... uh." I lift it for her to see. "I saw this at a yard sale this afternoon. I thought you'd—"

"I love it," she says, her gaze lifting to mine, and Jesus fuck, the genuine gratitude in her big brown eyes is like a fist to the gut.

"I thought you might. That's why I grabbed it. You love restoring old things, so..."

Okay, stop rambling, dude.

She runs her hand over the table top, her eyes full of admiration. "You actually picked this up for me?"

I shrug like it's no big deal, and it's not. We're friends. And friends buy each other things. Right? There was that time I purchased a ball cap for Kane when I was getting one for myself. Same deal.

She blinks up at me. "I don't know what to say."

"I do," her father says from behind.

My head lifts and for a moment there I forgot we weren't the only two people in the universe.

"You can tell me what's going on," he says with a chuckle.

Her face flushes and she looks so adorable all I want to do is lean in and kiss her.

"Dad I'm sorry. This is Rider, he's a friend of mine."

Her father shakes his head. "A friend? All this time you've been friends with The Wingman, and never thought to tell your old man, who's a big fan by the way."

"Sorry," Jules says with a sheepish grin. "Rider this is my dad, Jack."

I hold my hand out for a shake. "Nice to meet you, Jack."

Jack winks at Jules. "So when you say friend—"

"I mean friend," she says, her voice holding a measure of warning. "Don't get any ideas."

"Well it's nice to have friends who brings such thoughtful gifts."

"No, I'm going to pay for that," Jules says, and I stop her from turning.

"It's okay. I should go. You're busy with your family."

Before I know what's happening, Jack takes the table from me, sets it inside, and comes back to put his arm around my shoulders. He leads me down the hall, and into the kitchen where Jules' family are milling about, sipping wine, and chatting. All conversations come to a fast standstill when they see me.

"I shouldn't be intruding," I say and begin to back up, but come to a halt when I smack into Jules. Her hands go to my sides, and the warmth of her fingers seeps under my shirt and flows through my veins. Fuck, I love the way she touches me. I spin, and put my hands on her delicate shoulders. "I'm sorry. Are you okay?"

"I'm good," she says, her lips parted, her voice breathless, and it takes me back to our night in bed. Goddammit, I hated leaving her this morning. It took every ounce of strength I possessed not to wake her again and put my mouth all over her.

"I'll grab another plate," someone says from behind me, and Jules smiles.

"You're not getting out of this one, Wingman," she says.

I lower my voice for her ears only. "I didn't mean to interrupt."

"I know, but there are plenty of people here who are glad you did."

"Why?"

"Fishing for compliments?" she teases.

Yeah, maybe I am. Maybe I want to ask if she's happy I'm here.

The question sits on my tongue, but I don't vocalize it. I

don't want her to get the wrong idea, or the right idea, or...oh hell, I don't even know what is right or wrong anymore.

"Let's do this," she says.

"Mom, Dad, Misty, Jan, Lauren, Stacey, and Bella. This is Rider." She smiles at me, but there is a teasing warning in her eyes—that I'm about to be bombarded. "Rider, meet my family."

JULES

I just finish filling Peaches' food bowl when the text comes in.

Rider: Miss me?

I laugh and pick up my phone.

Jules: Like a hyena misses a toothache.

Rider: Hey!

Jules: Kidding.

After his away game last night, the guys went out to celebrate the win, but Rider went back to the room to Skype with me. It was another fun night, and as much as I hate to admit it, and would never voice a word of it to him, I miss him more than words can say.

Rider: What are you wearing?

Jules: Didn't we do this last night?

Rider: Yeah, that was fun, but I'm serious. I'll be there in ten minutes. Put on something comfortable, and warm. We're going out.

Jules: Where are we going?

Rider: You'll see.

I drop my phone and hurry upstairs to my room. My pulse

is leaping, anxious to feel his arms around me again. Yeah, okay, so I shouldn't be letting myself get carried away, shouldn't let myself fall for the man who's a sworn bachelor for life—a guy who thinks people love him because he's a hockey player.

Am I falling for him?

Oh, God, I very well could be and that frightens me more than anything. More than losing him? Honestly though, my time with him has been a whirlwind, and we've been having so much fun, I hadn't realized that I've been going through life without living it. Fear has been holding me back, but goddammit, I'm so tired of being afraid.

With my emotions in turmoil, I tug on a pair of yoga pants, a t-shirt and grab my favorite hoodie. The sound of his Jeep pulling into the driveway brings a big smile to my face. I glance at my reflection in the mirror, smooth my hair back, and walk down the stairs when all I want to do is run into his arms.

He knocks and I open the door. The sight of him, freshly showered, hair still damp, overwhelms me. "You still have my key, don't you?"

"Yeah," he says and steps in to me, until his hard body is pressed against mine. "Want it back?"

"No, it's always good for a friend to have a key." I give a casual shrug. "You know, in case I lock myself out." He nods, and I feel an odd little punch to my heart. What? Did I want him to say we were more than friends? Jesus, Jules, get it together. Things might be changing for you, but that doesn't mean they're changing for him.

"Or if I want to sneak in and ravish you."

"Yeah, that too," I say, working to keep my voice casual.

His cock thickens against my stomach and I reach between us and cradle it. His eyes briefly shuts and he groans. "Keep that up and we won't get out of here."

"Maybe I don't want to."

His eyes darken as his gaze moves over my face, and for a brief second, he looks like he's waging some internal war, then he exhales and steps back. "There are so many things I'm going to do to you later." Peaches steps up to us and curls around his legs.

"Looks like she's warming up to you."

"Or she's trying to trip me up."

I laugh. "Yeah, probably that."

"You ready?" he asks and takes my hands.

I fish my keys from my purse. "Are you going to tell me where were we're going?"

"Nope."

"As long as it's not a gum wall, I'm game."

He grins. "It's hard to beat the gum wall, but I think you'll like this."

We make our way to his Jeep and he opens the door to let me in. I buckle up and my heart squeezes as he circles the front of the vehicle, giving me a wicked grin. I have no idea where he's taking me, but I'm pretty sure I'd go anywhere with him tonight. Not a good thing, not a good thing at all.

His hand slides across the seat and captures mine. I turn his away and my heart is somewhere in my throat as I take in his smile.

"You liked the game last night?"

I roll my eyes. "It was okay. I only watched it because Dad made me. I never should have let him know we were friends."

"At least they didn't get the wrong idea about us."

"My sister was happy we were just friends. I think someone has a crush."

He grins, and it's so damn cute, I can't help but bring his hand to my mouth and kiss it. "Which one?" he asks.

"All of them." He laughs out loud.

"I told them you didn't date." I let out a playful sigh.

"You're a heartbreaker, Wingman, and it's hard to be your Wingwoman when I know it's never going to be long term. Women want that, you know?"

"Not you, though, right?"

I cast a fast glance his way, but he's scrubbing his chin and staring straight out the window. His concentration is so focused, you'd think the road ahead held all the answers to the universe.

"Ah, yeah, right," I say, my insides a bit shaky. Can he see through me? Does he know I'm falling for him? Will that be the end of us?

Dammit, I don't want it to be.

His smile dissolves. "So I should probably tell you..."

I frown and try to read him, but he won't look at me. "Tell me what?"

"You know our goaltender?"

"The guy they call the Puck Charmer?"

"And you say you're not a hockey fan," he says with a grin, but it's forced. I laugh at that. "Well, apparently, he's interested in you."

My head rears back. "In me?"

"Why do you say it like that?"

"I just...I don't think I'm his kind of girl."

"If you want me to be your Wingman, just let me know."

"Oh, okay," I say, and turn from him, incredulous that he's all game for setting me with up with a teammate. Then again, maybe it's a good damn reminder of what we are and what we aren't.

I reach for the radio and turn it up, wanting the music to drown the sounds of my swallowing. A short while later, Rider parks and I glance out the window to see the Space Needle, so beautifully lit up under the night sky. My heart is pounding overtime, and sweat breaks out on my hands.

"What are we doing here?" I ask, my voice breaking slightly.

"I thought it'd be fun. It's been a long time for me. I know you're not a thrill-seeker, so I wasn't about to take you skydiving, but this is pretty tame, right?" He winks at me. "Baby steps."

I take a deep breath, then another, and work to keep myself in check, but stupid tears pool in my eyes.

"Jules?" Rider asks, his voice so soft and worried, every emotion bottle up inside me bursts to the surface. "We don't have to do it."

"No, I should," I say.

His brows bunch and I turn from him. "You should?"

I sniff and he touches my chin to angle my face his way. "Hey, you can talk to me. If you're afraid—"

"This is the last place Brett and I went, before..."

I try to turn away again, but he unbuckles both of us and shifts until he's close. He doesn't speak, doesn't press and for that I'm grateful. I just let him hold me for a minute, and all around us, voices reach our ears as excited tourists make their way to the attraction.

"He was...my everything," I say quietly. I lean into him, absorb his comfort and warmth. His head nods against my shoulder. "I miss him."

"Tell me about him," he says quietly, and that brings a smile to my face, because while it's hard to talk about Brett, I like that he wants to hear.

"He was my first, you know. First everything."

His smile is sweet, and he brushes my hair back. "He was special to you."

"Very. We did everything together. We thought we would one day get married and have a family, but all that changed..."

I sniff, and Rider wipes at a loose tear.

"What happened?" he asks.

"Leukemia. Senior year of high school." I take a fueling breath and glance at the Space Needle. We came here prom night, and then he got too sick to leave the hospital. I've never had the courage to come back since."

"Tell me more about him," he says.

Before I realize what I'm doing, I'm sharing stories about Brett, things I've kept bottled up and never shared with another soul. Some make me laugh, others make me cry, but speaking them out loud somehow helps soothe my soul, mend the hole in my heart. As I continue to talk, Rider holds me, and his comfort means the world to me.

"Sounds like Brett and I would have gotten along."

"You would have loved him. Everyone did."

"I know I would have. I'm glad he got a chance to love you, Jules. The way you deserve to be loved."

I swallow against the tightness in my throat. "Thank you."

"Sometimes life just isn't fair," he says, and rakes his hand through his hair. "We just have to play the cards we're dealt."

"And keep on playing the game," I add.

He nods, and he looks through the window, but it's easy to tell his thoughts are a million miles away.

"You did good, Rider."

"What?" he says, my voice pulling him back.

"With the cards you were dealt. You did good."

He grunts a non-response, and says, "Come on, I'll take you home." He's about to move away, but I grasp his arm.

"No, I want to do this. Brett would want me to do this. He's probably tired of me being a—"

"Chickenshit."

I laugh at that, long and hard, and there is a new lightness in my shoulders when I stop. "I'm not sure I'd put it that way." I shake my head. "You really don't hold back anything, do you?" I say and nudge him.

"Yeah," he says and turns from me abruptly, so abruptly, it

takes me by surprise. Was it something I said? "You sure you want to do this?" he asks, as he looks out the driver's side window.

"I do," I say.

"Okay." We exit the Jeep and he puts his hand on the small of my back to lead me to the attraction. An hour later —yes, after an hour—we finally make it. It's not like we were far, or had to walk miles, but fans came out of the woodwork once they saw Rider. As he took pictures with his admirers, I stood back and watched. Is it any wonder he thinks the reason he's loved is because of his position on the Seattle Shooters? But he's so much more than a hockey player. He's a brother, a friend, a nurturer and protector. In fact, he's one of the best guys I know.

And I'm falling for him.

His arm circles my back as we take in the spectacular view, and while I thought it would be hard to come back to this place, with Rider by my side, holding me, I'm glad I did. In fact, I probably couldn't have done it without anyone but him by my side. After we make our way back to the street, we hold hands and quietly walk to his Jeep.

"Any other surprises?" I ask.

"Nope."

"I might have one," I say.

One brow raises. "Yeah?"

I give him a playful grin. "Or not!"

"You're a tease, you know that?"

"You think that's me teasing."

"Yeah, I do."

"Take me home, Rider. I'll show you teasing."

His eyes narrow in on me and the next thing I know, he's starting the Jeep and pulling into traffic. His knuckles are tight around the wheel but he's reining his speed in, for me.

But I'm just as anxious as he is, and maybe everything about this man creates an aura of safety.

"Can we go a little faster?" I say.

His gaze jerks to mine. "Yeah?" he asks, and I widen my legs, run my hands up my inner thighs. I'm pretty sure I've never wanted to be touched by this man more than I do at this moment.

"Yeah. Just don't speed. A ticket will only slow us down."

"Motherfucker," he says, his teeth sinking into his bottom lip as I caress my thigh. He goes a little faster, hits the speed limit and stays there and soon enough, he pulls into my driveway. We both hurry from the vehicle and like two teens with five minutes alone until their folks show up, we hurry to my door. I reach for my key, but he produces his faster and lets us in.

"I'm so glad I gave you that key," I say, and his lips find mine as we stumble inside. He closes the door, presses me against it and deepens the kiss. I moan against his lips and close my eyes, welcoming all the sensations. Peaches brushes against my leg and purrs.

"We have company," Rider murmurs into my mouth.

"Oh, shoot."

He backs up. "What?"

I glance up the steps, and then back at Rider. "I forgot to feed her."

"I'll do it," he says, falling right in to my trap.

I put my hand to his face. "Thanks. Oh, she has a special bag of treats in the closet too. Maybe you could give her one?" It's a small lie, but I need a bit of time.

"Sure," he says, adjusting his pants like he's in total agony.

"I'll meet you up there," I say, and dart upstairs to get ready. I rush to my room, peel off my clothes and slip into a short skirt. Excitement wells up inside me. Good Lord, never in the past would I have been so brazen, but this man brings out the naughty side in me, makes me feel safe and secure in opening myself up to him sexually.

What about emotionally?

Not wanting to think about that right now, I swipe a bit of lipstick across my lips, and when I hear Rider yelling up to me, I stifle a grin. I don't answer him, and he finally gives up calling and rushes up the stairs.

"Jules, I can't find...holy shit," he says, his voice raw and edgy when he finds me bent over the bed. Under the guise of fussing with the sheets, I offer my ass up to him.

"Can't find what?" I ask, and toss him a glance over my shoulder.

"Never mind." His nostrils flare as his eyes narrow in on me. For a split second I'm about to call abort, because I've never, ever seen such intensity on his face before. "Just found everything I've ever wanted."

My body pulses, the room growing hotter with the electricity arcing between us and since I've come too far to turn back now, I tug at the sheets and turn from him. He tears his shirt from his body, and it excites me even more.

"What are you talking about?" I ask, feigning innocence. "I'm just trying to tuck the corner of the bedding on here."

"Oh, is that what you're doing?"

"I haven't been able to get the sheets right since *you* messed them up." I make a tsking sound, like this is such a hard chore.

"Yeah, well. You should prepare yourself."

"Excuse me," I say doing my best to sound casual when my entire body is about to spontaneously combust.

"That's not all I'm going to mess up, babe."

"What are you talking about?"

"You can't bend over, looking like sex on the bed, without me reacting, but I think this is exactly what you were going for."

"Do you now. Know me that well?"

"Yeah, I do," he says and I'm not about to disagree. We've been sharing a lot, opening up to each other in so many ways, ways I'd be afraid to do with anyone but him. "You know me too."

It's true, I believe I do, but my mind shuts down when his hot hand presses against my spine, and he runs it down until he reaches my ass. I quiver under his direct touch, and my panties dampen even more. He's going to love finding them sopping wet and it makes me happy to please him.

"It's like fucking Christmas morning walking in here and finding you like this." He slides his finger under my skirt and lifts it. "All wrapped up like a perfect present."

"Now all you have to do is unwrap me," I say. "And then you get to play with me all night."

My words do something to him. He shoves my skirt up, and steps back. I wait for his touch but when it doesn't come, I look at him over my shoulder. His breathing is harsh, labored as his gaze focuses on my ass. I wiggle for him and he growls.

Needing, wanting him to touch me, I beg, "Rider."

His eyes finally lift, meet mine, and the lust reflected there weakens my body. "Yeah."

"Touch me, please."

He runs his warm palm over my ass, kneading me like I'm dough, and I moan in bliss. A second later he rips my lacy panties from my hips and I gasp when he grins at me.

"They were in the way," he says and slides one thick finger into me.

"Oh, God, yes."

"Up on your knees," he commands, and I do as he asks, until I'm down on all fours on the bed, his to do with as he pleases.

"Like this?" I ask.

"Exactly like that." He finger-fucks me for a few seconds, and pleasure centers in my core. His finger stills inside me and I whimper.

"Fuck my finger," he growls. I move back and forth on his finger and he slides a second one in. "You are so goddamn sexy, I'm going to lose it."

"I want your cock inside me," I murmur. "I want you to fill me and fuck me. Hard and soft. I want you to pound against me, burying yourself in me deep. I want you to make a goddamn mess of me, Rider," I say, my voice breathless as I lose myself in my need for this man.

"Yeah, that's it. Tell me everything."

I blink, hardly able to believe who I am with this man, but liking that girl very much. "I want it all and I want it now," I say.

"You're going to get it all. Before we're done, I'm going to fill you with my cum. I've already filled your sexy mouth, and your sweet cunt, now it's time for me to fill you here," he says, as he probes my back opening. I gasp and stop moving and his hand stills. My mind races. I've never had anal sex before. Never wanted to, but with Rider, I want to experience it all. As my mind settles on the idea, I begin moving again, encouraging him to pick up where he left off.

He's a bit hesitant at first, but when I wiggle my ass, searching for his thumb, he circles my puckered opening.

"Yes," I say, and he groans.

"You're killing me, babe. My cock is so goddam hard. I'm fucking hurting."

"I can kiss it better."

His hand circles my body, presses against my clit, and in seconds flat the world disappears from my vision. I give over to the sensations, and a hot burst of heat floods my sex and pours from my trembling body. Rider leans over me, his entire being absorbing my convulsions, and anchoring me to him as I ride out the waves. God, I love the way he makes me feel so safe.

"I love when you let go and come like that. It's so damn beautiful."

I gasp for breath, and he circles my clit, his thumb still in my backside. I glance at him over my shoulder, take in his pants. "You're way overdressed. I want you naked, now," I demand.

His grin is wicked, as one brow arches at my command, but it's easy to tell he likes it when I'm bossy. Well then...

"All you had to do was ask."

"I just did. So get on with it." His chuckle reverberates through me, and I move forward on the bed. His fingers fall from my sex, and I miss his touch already as I turn to sit on the bed. "I want your cock right here," I say and take one of his fingers and slide it into my mouth. I taste myself on his finger as I suck and he groans as his head falls back.

"You are so good at that."

A thread of satisfaction weaves its way through me and feeds my desire. I reach for his pants, and open his button and zipper and struggle to get them down. His finger plops from my hungry mouth to shove his pants down his legs. He gets them to his ankles, uses his heels to remove them and kicks them away.

"Clothes are so damn overrated," he teases as he steps up to me, taking his cock into his hand to rub. My gaze drops to it. I want to be the one exploring his erection again with my hands and mouth.

"In fact," he says. "When we're here, I think we should have a new rule. No clothes at all."

I grin at him and almost forget how to breathe, but when I take in a breath, the scent of his skin curls around me. My entire body heats all over again. How will I ever make it out of this affair in one piece? Yeah, he's made a mess of me, but

I can't say he hadn't warned me—or that I hadn't asked him to.

"I'm not going to argue with that," I say, working hard to rein myself in as I become aware of his entire body—every beautiful inch of it. "But I'd like to wear them while I'm cooking. I'm not a thrill-seeker like you."

He wets his finger and brushes it over my bottom lip like he's preparing me for his fat cock, but I'm ready. I am so ready.

"You're a little more adventurous than you think, Jules," he whispers, his warm breath falling over me.

I smile up at him. I like the idea of that. "Well, let's see how adventurous I can be right now," I say and lean forward to lick the pre-cum pooling on his crown.

"Motherfucker," he growls and grips my hair and tugs. Who knew hair pulling could be so erotic? The things this man has taught me.

I moan, loving the taste of him on my tongue, the way he fills my mouth, widening my jaw almost to the point of pain. I take him deep and relax my throat to take even more and his heated curses fill me with pleasure. He grows in my mouth, his veins filling with heated blood as he rocks into me.

"Jules, my god, Jules, that mouth of yours."

His voice is deep, tortured and I slide my hands around his body and cup his perfect ass. He's so close I can almost taste his release on my tongue, but he inches back and his dark gray eyes meet mine.

"I need to be inside you," he says with a calm that belies his shaking body. I don't answer, instead I nod and shimmy back on the bed. "Lubricant?" he asks, and I know exactly what he has in mind.

"Drawer," I say.

He pulls open the drawer and does a quick scan of my

toys before snatching the lubricant. "If I knew you had these, I would have asked you to use them when we Skyped."

"Why bother Skyping? I can do it right here with you in the room."

His chuckle is hoarse and edgy. "You are such a fucking tease. Now get to the middle of the bed, and spread your legs for me."

I position myself and widen my thighs, welcoming him into my body as he grabs a condom from his pants. He sheaths himself, and climbs over me. His lips settle over mine, his tongue soft and probing at first, but becoming more urgent as I wrap my legs around him and lift my hips, taking him deep inside me.

"Yes," I moan into his mouth and stroke his back as he powers into me, each hungry thrust pulling another orgasm from me until I'm bursting all around him again.

"Baby, I feel you. You're so hot and wet around my cock."

"I love your cock," I murmur, and ride him until my orgasm subsides. The second I stop clenching, he pulls out and I grumble my disappointment. But a yelp escapes me when he flips me over and positions a pillow under my body, raising my ass to him.

"This will be a first for you," he says, a statement not a question, but I nod in response anyway. "Fuck baby, the way you trust me with your body..."

I glance over my shoulder and his eyes are pinched tight, and his head is shaking back and forth as he scrubs his chin like I'd just given him the greatest gift in the world. My heart tumbles, reaches out to him, allows him inside—and holy hell, I can't deny that I'm frightened by all the things this man makes me feel.

His eyes fly open, and zero in on my face. "I won't hurt you."

"I know," I say and lay my face on the pillow, gifting him a part of me I've never gifted another—and will never, ever give another. This is for Rider only.

He pours a generous amount of lubricant onto my opening, and spends a long time preparing me. I squirm, grow restless.

"Baby, I'm not taking you before you're ready."

"I am ready," I counter, although I'm not sure I was ever ready for a guy like him. He works me with his finger, and while he's trying to go slow, there is a new sense of urgency about it. I feel it too.

He finally, finally, presses his crown to my opening and I move, working to force him inside until I feel a sharp pain.

"Breathe, baby. Relax," he says. I take a breath and he adds, "Put your fingers between your legs, and rub your clit."

I rub myself, my mind on meltdown as sensations gather, curl in on me, and burst out from my core. He falls over my back, our wet bodies fusing together.

"I'm inside," he says, his hot breath spilling over my back and warming all my cold places. But it's not like he has to tell me, I feel every inch of him in my body. "Are you doing okay?"

I love his check in. "Yes," I murmur around the lump in my throat, and move against him, my actions louder than words. He moves with me, and it's beautiful the way he's caring for me, running his hand along my back in a soothing manner.

"I wish you could see, babe. The way you take me is un—fucking—believable."

"Tell me," I say.

"Your body opened right up for me. Every time I sink in to you, and you squeeze around me, it's...perfect." he says and tears fill my eyes. There is no way he can't be experiencing the same need, want...love...I'm feeling. "You're perfect."

I rub my clit harder, but it's his words that send me over

the precipice. I let go and he groans as my body tightens around his cock.

"Yes," he grunts, his fingers biting into my hips for leverage as he lets go high inside me. Happy tears prick my eyes and I swallow a cry as he completely collapses on top of me, his weight pinning me, comforting me, shielding me from the world.

We stay like that for a long time, and once I'm able to breathe again, he rolls off me. He disposes of the condom, crawls back in beside me and covers us with the sheets. He's quiet, maybe too quiet, and reflective. I want to ask what's on his mind, but I'm almost afraid to. His breathing is still ragged, like his adrenaline hasn't receded—like he's in fight or flight mode.

He pulls me to him and places his hand on my chest. "Your heart is still pounding as hard as mine. Breathe with me," he says and puts his forehead to mine. We don't break eye contact as we take deep breaths and let them out slowly, and the moment is so intimate, maybe more intimate than anything we did so far, I fear there might not be a way to come back from it if he's not on the same page as I am.

His throat works as he swallows and he shifts beside me, putting his arm on his head and angling me on his body so I can't see his face.

"I'm having a surprise party for Kane this weekend," he says, his voice flat, maybe a bit despondent.

"Lindsay mentioned it," I say. Where is he going with this? Is he inviting me, ready to introduce me to his friends? Why does he sound so unamused? Lindsay said he was excited to surprise his brother—who swore he didn't want a party.

"Yeah, I needed her help to get him there."

"Right," I say. "Kane's in good hands with Lindsay."

His hand drops from his forehead, his fingers brushing along my arm. "I'd...like for you to come," he says.

My pulse jumps. Does this mean he *is* ready to introduce me to his friends, that he might feel more than friendship for me, too? "Ah, are you sure?"

"Yeah, Alek will be there."

Beneath my cheek, his heart picks up pace again. "What?" I ask, not understanding what he's saying. I lift my head to see him, and that damn dimple is back.

"I think you two should meet. I'll set it up." He winks at me. "Then you'll see this Wingman's got game."

"I'm not going," I say to Lindsay as I press my cell to my ear harder, and pace restlessly around my bedroom. Peaches meows and weaves her way between my legs. Maybe I'll get lucky, fall down the stairs, and end up in traction. That would certainly provide a solid excuse for avoiding Kane's surprise party at Rider's place.

My God, I was ready to lay my feelings on the line after lovemaking—correction, after sex. It's a good thing I didn't. I scoff. Yeah, a really good thing I didn't considering he's all game to set me up with someone else. But after being with Rider, I realized I was tired of being afraid, tired of going through the motions of living without actually living. He's opened my eyes to so many things, taught me how to live and love again. Now, well, I don't want to be afraid of everything anymore. I want to live life...I want to love. Brett would want that for me too.

Peaches cries louder, and if I didn't know better, I'd think she was missing Rider as much as me. I steal a quick glance at my neatly made bed. It's been days since he's been in it, days since I've heard from him. No call, no text, no Skype. Not a single…anything. Yes, I get he's busy with hockey and practice, but still…

"Why don't you want to go?" she asks, pulling my focus back.

My heart cracks a little more as I grip my ponytail and tug, but that only reminds me of my time in bed with Rider. Oh Rider, why did you have to be so sweet and make me fall for you? I swallow a humorless laugh. This isn't on him. He told me he didn't do relationships right from the start, and I went and fell for him anyway. But I can't tell Lindsay that's the reason I don't want to go to the party. She'd warned me early on, and I straight up told her I knew what I was doing. The last thing I need is a lecture from her right now, even though it'd be well-meaning and caring because she only has my best interests at heart.

"I have a migraine coming on."

"Oh really. I'm so sorry to hear that."

I feel crappy for lying, and hey, maybe I'll get lucky and wind up in bed with a killer headache before the end of the night.

"Can you take some meds and rest?" she asks, dishes clanging in the background.

"Yeah, I suppose."

"Are you sure you're okay? You sound…strange."

"Headache," I remind her and curse myself for letting my voice wobble. It's going to take extra effort to keep the truth from my friend.

"Well, I'm sure it will be gone by tomorrow. I really *need* you at the party, Jules," she says, an almost pleading tone in her voice.

"Why?" I pace to my window, stare out at the dark night and then flop onto my bed.

"Because…I…uh…I'm meeting all the hockey players and their wives. I can't do that without you by my side."

"Since when?" I blurt out. My God, she's outgoing, flamboyant and a great conversationalist. Everything I'm not. If anything, it should be me asking her to hold my hand.

"I like this guy. I want to make a good impression."

I snort. "Then you should leave me home."

"Come on. I know Rider asked you to go. He told Kane. It must mean he wants to introduce you to his friends."

Oh, he does. To one friend, anyway. Some goaltender named Alek. Aka the Puck Charmer. Yeah, awesome. Exactly the kind of guy I'd go for. You'd think Rider would know better. But I guess maybe he doesn't know me as well as I thought he did.

"We're just friends," I remind her.

"Please, Jules. Kane and I will pick you up. Oh, that's it," she says quickly. "I was trying to figure out how to get him to Rider's place without being suspicious." She gives a little squeal. "What I'll do is tell him we're going on that double date we talked—"

"Rider and I aren't dating."

"Anyway," she continues, ignoring me. "I'll tell him we're driving, and have to pick you up. This is perfect."

"Except I don't want to go."

"Please, for me," she begs in that whiny voice that truly is giving me a headache. Awesome.

I roll on my bed, and even though I washed the sheets, I can still smell Rider's scent. As I listen to Lindsay beg, I shut my eyes. For the life of me, I can't understand why she's so desperate for me to go. She's quite capable of functioning in a crowd without me. I have no doubt everyone will fall in love with her and welcome her into their tightly knit group.

"Can I let you know tomorrow?" I say.

"Yeah, sure. We'll pick you up at eight," she announces, taking my answer as a yes. "Wear that cute blue dress we got from Westers."

"Now you're dressing me?"

"I want you to look your best."

"Why?" My God, who is this woman and what has she done with my best friend?

"I don't know. I'm just nervous, okay?"

Honestly, I've never seen her like this before. Things must be pretty serious between her and Kane. I groan and toss on my bed. If my best friend needs me, I can't let her down. We're there for each other, and when I lost Brett, and was ridiculed by Jason, she was left to put the pieces back together. How can I not be at her side when she asks so little from me?

"See you at eight," I say, and I can almost picture her throwing her hands up in victory. "Now I'm going to go and get a good night's sleep."

"Thanks, babe," she says and I swipe my finger across the screen to end the call. I check one more time to see if there is anything from Rider, and my stomach falls when there's nothing. I toy with my phone, and almost send off 'karaoke', but toss my phone before I go through with it.

I toss and turn and the next thing I know, morning is upon me. I pull myself out of bed, and glance down at Peaches, who is sauntering into my room. I laugh. "Well, Peaches, it looks like it's just you and me girl. I'm going to become that crazy cat lady far before my time."

Peaches meows, rubs up against me and jumps into bed, curling up where the man I'm in love with had recently been.

"Yeah, I know. He grows on you."

I head downstairs, make myself a huge pot of coffee and spend the better part of the day doing chores. In my quiet house, which seems deafening without Rider's presence, I make myself something to eat, and sit at the table to eat, despite the fact that I've not had an appetite in days. By the time I look at the clock, it's nearing six, and my stomach lurches. Lindsay and Kane will be here in less than two hours and I'm not so sure I'm ready to come face to face with Rider. Or worse, have him try to set me up with his buddy. I want to bail, wish I could bail, but I can't do that to Lindsay.

I force myself into the shower, and tonight, instead of tying my hair back, the way Rider likes, I use the flat iron and smooth it out. I also put on makeup, more than I normally would, and tug on the dress Lindsay suggested. I take a glance at myself in the mirror and smile. I clean up pretty good, and look nothing like the girl Rider first met.

Wait.

Oh God, am I dressing up and caking on the makeup because...because I want to look more like the girls he's normally attracted to? Crap. I rush to the bathroom, and wash my face clean, until my cheeks are red and rubbed raw.

Girl, you are in so much trouble.

The doorbell rings and my dinner rises in my throat. "Okay, Jules. You can do this for Lindsay." I stare at myself in the mirror, swipe lipstick across my lips and saunter downstairs, even though my knees are rubbery.

I pull open the door and plaster on a smile. Lindsay frowns at me. Goddammit, I hate how well she can read me.

"What?" I ask and glance down at the dress I'm wearing. Anything to avoid eye contact. "I'm wearing what you suggested."

"Have you been crying?" she asks, and worries her bottom lip.

"No, of course not. I just got soap in my eye when I showered."

"Okay, good. You have nothing to be sad about. I want you to know that."

"Uh, okay," I say, having no idea what she's talking about.

"Okay, good. Come on. Tonight is going to be a huge surprise for you."

"You mean for Kane."

"Yeah, exactly. That's exactly what I mean. I'm just all weirdly nervous tonight."

"It's just a surprise birthday party," I say with a shrug, my voice low so Kane doesn't here. She goes still and looks at me for a moment. She might know me, but I know her too.

"Do you have something you want to tell me?" I ask.

She shakes her head quickly. "No." Okay, now she's the one avoiding eye contact, but I don't have time to question her on that. She's darting down the steps. I lock up and follow her to Kane's sports car.

"You look gorgeous, by the way," she says to me.

"Thanks, you do too, and you have nothing to be nervous about. Everyone will love you."

"You have nothing to be nervous about either," she says again.

"I'm not nervous."

"Oh, okay."

I slide into the back seat. "Hey Kane. Nice to see you again."

"Jules," he says and glances over his shoulder to give me a big smile. I try not to fidget in the back seat as he negotiates traffic and pulls up in front of Rider's house. House? Okay, more like big-ass mansion. The driveway is empty and there isn't a vehicle on the street. Everyone must have parked elsewhere to keep the surprise.

We wait for a second, and Kane shoots off a text. He checks his phone. "He's running late and said for us to come in. Front door is open."

We all climb from the car and I follow the two up. Lindsay casts me a glance over her shoulder and I smile at her. Yup, I'm good. I'll make an appearance and as soon as she's comfortable, I'll get an Uber home. I just pray Rider is too busy with his brother and forgets his lame idea about setting me up.

Kane enters the dark house, and he flicks on the light. Dozens of people jump out at us and yell surprise. Kane curses and falters backward, and Lindsay laughs and hugs him. He hugs her back and the affection between the two warms me. They might be the real deal, and I'm not jealous at all.

Nope, not at all.

Or much.

I scan the crowd, check out all the smiling faces, and my stomach tightens when I see Rider. He's not looking at his brother. No, he's looking at me, and the intensity in his gaze robs me of my next breath.

"You bastard," Kane says, and shakes his head. "I told you I didn't want a party."

Rider makes his way through the crowd, hands Kane a beer and slaps him on the back. "The role of a big brother is to piss off his little brother, is it not?"

The two hug, and my heart pinches. They break apart and Kane introduces Lindsay to everyone. I hang back as they greet her, and wonder exactly what I should be doing. Soon enough, Rider is beside me.

"Hey," he says quietly, a voice reserved for the bedroom that does ridiculous things to me. "Drink?"

"Yes please," I say, needing one or a dozen.

His gaze moves over my face, and honest to God if I didn't know better, I'd think he felt the same way about me as I do about him. But I do know better, right? I mean, he talked about setting me up with his friend. Maybe we need to talk. Really talk. His childhood was rough, getting tossed around from house to house and yes, he's a grown man, but maybe that frightened boy still exists somewhere deep inside.

"Your friends seem nice," I say quietly.

"Let's get you a drink and I'll introduce you."

"Okay," I say. Rider wants to introduce me to all his friends? They'll probably all get the wrong idea—we both know that. Hell, we talked about that. Does that mean he's okay with that? Oh God, am I making more of this than I should? Is it just wishful thinking on my part?

We make our way to the kitchen. "Your home is beautiful," I say. "I like the color scheme."

"Liar," he says and I laugh, some of the tension easing from my body.

"I don't lie," I say.

"Then tell me what you really think."

Oh, how I want to open my mouth and do just that. How I want to confess my feelings, and throw myself at him, but I'm not sure his kitchen, during Kane's party is the right place for it. No, I'll have to get him alone before this night is over.

"Well," I say falling back into our easy way. "I do like the gray, but I might lighten it up a bit, and I have this really great table I plan to paint and that would look so good in your living room."

He grins. "That was a gift. You can't give that away."

"You're right. I do love it."

I smile at him, and he dips his head, his smile so sweet and genuine I almost forget that we're not back at my place, ready to slide between the sheets.

He touches my hair, runs it between his fingers. "I like your hair like this. You're beautiful." But then he frowns. "All the single guys—" He closes his mouth when a couple of women wander into the kitchen, but they're busy chatting and don't pay us too much attention as they refill their cups.

I wait for him to continue. When he doesn't, I say, "You look great too, Rider." I let my gaze slide down him, take in his button-down shirt and khaki pants.

"Listen...I...uh...about..." I hold my breath, and hope he's changed his mind about setting me up. I hope he's changed his mind about a lot of things, but then he closes his eyes, and wobbles a little bit.

I grab him. "Are you okay?"

After a moment, he opens his eyes. "Fine. I've just been having these dizzy spells."

"Rider, that's not good," I say as I try to examine his pupils.

He shakes his head and throws his hands up in the air. "Nurses!"

"Hockey players!" I exclaim.

"You got something against hockey players?" someone asks from behind.

I turn, and come face to face with some guy I don't know. "You going to introduce me to your friend or what?" he asks, flashing me a bright smile that undoubtedly turns women to dim witted moths.

"This is Jules," Rider says, his voice tight. "Jules, this is Alek."

My head bobs back and forth between Rider and Alek. Is this really happening? The man I love is actually going to go through with setting me up? Ground, please open up and swallow me whole.

"I haven't seen you at these parties before," Alek says, his voice a bit slurred as he comes closer.

"No, it's my first time," I say. "My friend Lindsay is dating Kane."

"Oh, I like her. Wait, you're not dating this douche bag, are you?" he asks, a teasing edge to his voice.

"Yeah, I mean..." I take in Rider's dark expression, and wait for him to intervene. When he doesn't, I say, "No."

"Come on then, let's go get to know each other better," he says, and puts his arm around my back. We head toward the doorway and my stomach is so tight and uneasy, I fear I'm going to lose my dinner.

"Alek, don't." Before I realize what's happening, Rider is shoving Alek away, and Alek's drink sloshes over the side of his glass.

"What the fuck, dude?" Alek says, and sets his drink on the counter. He shakes the beer from his hand.

"Back off," Rider says his voice holding all kinds of warnings.

"Listen, you've been riding my ass all week, and I don't fucking know why. You've got something to say to me, then say it already."

"Really, are you that fucking dense?" Rider asks, and shoves him again, but Alek isn't about to let anyone push him around. He shoves Rider back, hard, and he stumbles. Before I can catch him, he goes down, his head hitting the chair on the way. He lands with a thud, and those around us shriek.

Going into professional mode, even though my insides are screaming right along with those other girls, I drop to my knees and check his vitals. I glance up to see Kane and Lindsay standing over me, their eyes wide with worry.

I swallow the lump in my throat. "Call 911!"

14

RIDER

With my head throbbing like I'd just taken a hard one to the boards, I peel my eyes open, and look at my unfamiliar surroundings. Kane comes into view. Correction. Two Kanes come in to view and I close one eye to cure my double vision.

"Dude, what the fuck?" I ask and make a move to get up.

"Oh no you don't," he says and places his beefy palm on my shoulder to push me back down.

I squint and work to figure out what's going on. "Where am I?"

"Seattle General," he says.

"Why am I here?" I wrack my brain. The last thing I remember was shoving Alek after he tried to walk away with Jules.

"Where's Jules?" I ask.

"She was here a few minutes ago. She's working."

"Working?" I try to get up again but he stops me. "How long have I been here?"

"Since last night."

"Jesus. I need to get out of here. I need to find Jules. I have to talk to her."

"Yeah you do, but first you need to rest."

"I don't need to rest." I turn my head and nearly vomit when the room spins. "Oh shit, where's Alek? I owe that motherfucker a beat down."

"You don't owe him anything. He never did a thing to you."

"Jules—"

"He has nothing to do with Jules," he says, but I know him well enough to know he's keeping something from me.

"What's going on?"

"He never wanted to go out with Jules." He rakes his hair from his forehead. "I lied about that and put him up to taking Jules away from you at the party. Lindsay and I were both in on it."

"I don't get it," I say, my too tired brain unable to put the pieces together. "Where's Jules?" Right now, even though I have no idea what is going on, or why I'm in a hospital bed, the only one I want to talk to is my friend, my bedmate, the woman I love, but she's nowhere to be found.

"Wow, you're worse than I thought," he says, his voice full of worry. "You asked me that less than a minute ago and I told you she was working."

"I'm fine. I just want to talk to Jules." Before he can answer, a movement at the door gains my attention. I lift my eyes slowly, and my heart pounds harder. "Jules," I say quietly, no longer able to fight off my feelings for her. Seeing Alek's arm around her was like a hard slap to the face—the goddamn wakeup call that I actually needed.

Wait, why isn't she coming closer? Why is she hovering over there in the corner like I might have the plague?

Kane glances at her over his shoulder. "I think I'll give you two some space."

Jules gathers the bottom of her scrub top into her palms. And fusses with the hem. She looks everywhere and anywhere but at me.

"You okay?" I ask and hold a hand out to her, but she doesn't reach for it. Instead, she takes a step toward the door, like prey ready to flee.

"How are you feeling?" she asks, her gaze finally meeting mine.

"Like I just got run over by a truck."

"That bad, huh?" Her big brown eyes are wide, like a damn deer in the headlights. "The doctor will be here in a minute to talk to you."

I touch my head, wince when I feel the bump. "Dammit, I though Alek only shoved me, but now I'm thinking he has one hell of a good left hook."

"When you fell, you hit the chair." She snaps her fingers. "You went out like that. I thought...I was...this isn't your first concussion," she says, her shaky words alluding to something, but my head is pounding so hard I can't quite figure out what is going on.

A woman in a white coat enters and walks up to my bed. "Glad to see you're finally awake."

She pulls a pen light from her pocket and flicks it over my eyes. I wince. She turns her attention to my file and jots down a few notes. "We're going to run a few more tests."

"I don't have time for that," I say and try to push the blanket off me. The room tumbles before my eyes and the doctor puts her hand on me to settle me back on the bed. I try to shake it off, a measure of panic welling up inside me. This can't be happening. This *isn't* happening. "I need to hit the rink. We have a game coming up."

Her lips pinch as she frowns, and she nods slowly, like she's placating me. "I'm afraid you won't be playing so soon. Your teammates have been here all night, and your brother

Kane has already talked to your coach. You have swelling, and need rest."

I pinch the bridge of my nose. "Jesus Christ, is this some kind of a joke?"

"It's not a joke, Mr. Lewis. Concussions are very serious and not something we take lightly here at Seattle General. Your team will have to get by without you, I'm afraid."

"Not happening," I say but collapse onto the bed when the room fades to a dark shade of gray. The doctor makes a few more notes, and stops at the door to talk to Jules. Her voice is low, and I don't have the energy to strain to hear. I take a breath, then another. How the fuck is this happening? I have to play, hockey is my life...it's my everything. Its why people like me.

It's not why Jules likes you.

My heart crashes harder at that thought. Honest to God, I'm in love with a woman who cares nothing about hockey and I can't fight it anymore—don't want to fight it anymore. She's a kind, caring woman who is brilliant, beautiful and fills my heart with hope and love. She's everything to me, and has given my life a new purpose. I want to make her happy, want to see her smile every day, want to take care of her needs, and be a part of her big family. In fact, I want to start a family with her. But what does she want? I study her body language, the way she's turned from me—a cold chasm between us— and a measure of unease creeps into my veins.

Okay, if she doesn't care about hockey, why then, after finding out I can't play, is she acting so distant? Jesus Christ, was she fucking with me? Pretending to dislike the game, when in reality it means as much to her as it does to her father? And now that I'm benched, for fuck knows how long, she's distancing herself.

Is this really fucking happening?

Every worry, every old insecurity comes rushing back in a

flurry, and once again, I'm reduced to that young boy nobody wanted, that parentless hellion who was unlovable. I breathe, but it feels like fire in my chest as I fill my aching lungs. My heart pounds harder, raw against my ribcage until the room closes in on me. I lower my lids, and work to sort through everything that's happened in the last couple weeks.

"Your family is here to see you," Jules says, after the doctor leaves.

"Jules..." I croak out.

"I have another patient I need to check on," she says.

"You mean torture," I tease, a last-ditch effort to make things right between us. I search her face, search for a nugget that tells me I'm wrong here—that there is more between us and she wants to act on it as much as I do. She steps back, widening the chasm between us. Fuck, she might as well have slammed me into the boards. Okay, I get it. I get where we stand.

The empty sensation in my stomach climbs higher, and bile punches into my throat. I love this woman, and I have to make this easy on her.

"So, you and Alek," I begin. Wait, what was that Kane said about him setting it up. I try to quiet my trembling brain and figure it out, but can't.

"Rider," she begins. "I don't want to go out with Alek."

"Oh, okay then. Well, when I'm feeling better we can hit up Nelly's, and I'll resume my wingman duties." Her body goes perfectly still, and I'm not even sure she's breathing. "Jules?"

"Yeah, okay. Sounds great," she says, and the next thing I know, she's gone from my room and likely my life.

I put my hand over my head, my heart somewhere in the vicinity of my throat. Everything inside me hurts, and it's not from my concussion. No, it's because my career could very well be over, but more importantly, the woman I love doesn't feel the same way about me as I do about her. Each breath rakes fire across my chest, and I fight the tears so hard they pound behind my eyes.

"Mom and Dad are here to see you," Kane says and I open my eyes to see him and Lindsay coming into the room.

Keep it together, Rider.

Behind my bro and his girlfriend, I spot Marion and Arthur. Water pools in Marion's eyes, and Arthur has his arm around her, supporting her like the great husband he is. Honestly, he's shown us all what it's like to be a good husband and a good father—something I desperately needed in my young life.

"Hey," I say and try to inject a bit of enthusiasm into my voice.

Marion hurries to me. "Rider, we were so worried."

"I'm okay," I lie, knowing I'll never be okay again.

Marion hugs me, and Arthur puts his hand on my shoulder. "You gave us a good scare there, son."

"Sorry about that."

He laughs. "When they release you, why don't you come home with us? Marion will nurse you back to health in no time, and you'll be back on the ice before you know it."

I try to swallow the lump in my throat but can't get it down. "What if I'm not?"

Arthur frowns as Kane pulls a chair up for his mother to sit. "What are you talking about?"

I turn from him. "Doc says I'll likely be out for the rest of the season. Maybe forever...who knows."

"Shit," Kane says under his breath.

Yeah, shit...

"I know hockey means everything to you, Rider," Marion says. "But your health is much more important to all of us."

"What?" I ask, and turn to her, but when I do, the room spins.

"Easy, bro," Kane says.

I pinch the bridge of my nose. "Marion?"

"Yes," she says quietly.

"What if...what if I never play again?"

"Then you find something else to do," she says, like it's an easy solution. "No matter what, we'll be here to support you in whatever you decide."

"Yeah?" I ask, my hands as shaky as my body as I rake my fingers through my hair.

"Of course we will," Jaclyn says as she comes rushing in, Lucy behind her. I stare at my two younger sisters and take in Jaclyn's snarl. "If you didn't have a concussion, I'd smack you," she says. She's the one who's always understood that I never truly felt like I was family.

"Why are you always hitting me?" I grouch.

"Because I'm your younger sister, and you're my big stupid older brother. No matter what, family supports each other, and yes, Rider, you *are* family. When are you going to finally start believing that?"

"Hear how she talks to me," I say to Marion who is laughing softly, but my heart is racing with the things I feel for this family. My family.

"Hey Lucy," I say as she bends to give me a hug. She rubs her big tummy as she stands back up. "How are you feeling?"

"Better than you." I laugh at that. "Now you need to rest because this little one wants her uncle healthy and happy when she's born."

Uncle.

"You guys really don't care if I can never play again?" Honestly, how the fuck did I get so lucky?

"Oh, my God, I am going to smack you," Jaclyn says and it brings a big smile to my face.

"Me too," Lindsay says quietly and I look at her. Jesus, if

looks could kill, I'd be six feet under. What did I ever do to her?

Kane sits on the edge of my bed. "Dude, you're family. No matter what."

"We love you for you, you big dummy," Jaclyn says with an exaggerated eye roll.

I take in all eyes staring at me, and tears prick my eyes. "I couldn't have asked for a better family," I say my heart aching, for the people I have here, and for the girl I've lost. Marion was wrong when she said hockey was everything to me. It might have been, but as I take in all the concerned faces, I realize there is more to life than the game. More to me than my skills.

"We should let you rest," Kane says, and everyone nods in agreement.

I get a dozen kisses from the girls and everyone files out, everyone except Lindsay, who is staring at me, her arms folded, anger in her eyes.

"Uh, everything okay?" I ask.

"Of course not." She steps closer. "What did you say to Jules?"

"I..." God, just hearing her name is ripping me wide open. "What are you talking about?"

"She left your room crying."

My pulse jumps and I try to sit up. "I...why was she crying?"

"You obviously said something to hurt her?"

"I'd never do anything to hurt her, Lindsay. I love her," I blurt out without thinking.

"I know you do," she says, and Kane comes back into the room.

"We all know you do," he says.

I frown. "You do?"

"Of course," Lindsay says, exasperated. "That's why Kane and I let you believe Alek was interested in her."

"I don't get it."

"No surprise there," Lindsay says, and shakes her head. Okay I get it she thinks I'm dense, and I can't disagree with her on that one. "Look, Rider. You love her, she loves you and we had to do something to push you both past your fears so you'd fight for each other."

Sweat breaks out on my body. "What?" I ask, as my mind slows, the tumblers falling into place. "Oh, shit." I've spent years feeling like an outsider in Kane's family, thinking that I was only loved because of hockey. But Jules, well, Jules loved and lost, and has demons of her own.

"She loves you, Rider," Lindsay says quietly. "Seeing you like this scared her half to death, but I know she's tired of being afraid. She's ready to take a chance on life, a chance on love...a chance on you."

"I fucked everything up."

"Yeah, you did."

I lay back and stare at the ceiling. "She must hate me."

"Then go fix it," Kane says.

15

JULES

"Why are we here?" I groan and glance around Nelly's bar, which is crazy busy tonight. For a second, I think I see one of Rider's teammates and then another. I must be hallucinating. I've never seen them here before, so why would they all show up tonight? Honestly though, this is the last place I want to be. It reminds me too much of Rider and all the great times we had together. That man...the things he did to me, taught me, the way I opened up under his care.

Get it together, girl.

"Because I'm tired of you moping around your place." Lindsay toys with her straw. "You need to get out and meet people...meet guys."

"I don't want to meet anyone," I say. How can Lindsay possibly think I can go out with a guy when my heart belongs to another? It's been a week—the longest week of my life—since Rider woke up in that hospital bed. The doctors had run some tests, and chances are he's home by now. Not that I know for certain, and I'm not about to ask Lindsay. After he was admitted, I took a much-needed vacation—I just couldn't face him every day after he pushed me away. As he rested, his team played their next game without him, and won. I'm thankful for that and I really hope Rider gets a clean bill of health so he can play the season's last few games. I know how important hockey is to him. It comes before everything else.

"How about that guy over there?" Lindsay says and points to Tate. "He looks like your type."

"Rider's his type," I say, and curse myself for saying his name out loud, for loving the way it sounds on my tongue.

Lindsay makes a face. "Huh?"

"Rider was my wingman, remember?" I remind her. "He set me up with that guy and all he did was talk about Rider until I sent our safe word."

"Safe word?"

"If a date went bad, we texted 'karaoke' to each other. Rider was big on safety." I smile and then shake it off. I need to stop thinking about him for my own mental health. I take a huge drink of my wine and nearly finish it off in record time.

"Kane's here," Lindsay says and waves him over.

I'm not too worried about Rider being with him. No way would he be up and out this soon. He took one hell of a hit to the head. Lindsay stands and gives Kane a kiss and my heart pinches. I'm so happy for them.

"Hey Jules," Kane says, and plops down next to me.

"Kane," I say and force a smile.

"So you and Alek," he says and Lindsay gives him a grin.

Oh hell no! This has to stop and has to stop now.

"There is no me and Alek."

"Yet," he says. "He's here, a bunch of guys from the team are, and I thought I'd be your wing man."

"No, please, don't."

Before I can stop him, he stands and speaks to someone

behind me. Mortified, I hunch forward and stare at the few drops left in my drink, willing all this to just go away.

"So yeah," he says to whoever it is hovering close. "I've found myself with two women tonight, and since I'm a one girl kind of guy, I thought you might like to help me out."

"Ground open up and swallow me whole," I murmur. I play with my phone, and resist the urge to type out 'karaoke.' That thought makes me laugh. Rider is laid up and not about to come to my rescue. Heck, maybe I should go out with other guys, maybe that will help me forget Rider once and for all.

"You've got no game, bro," the familiar voice says from behind.

I stand so fast, my chair topples and Rider grabs it. He moves it aside so there is nothing between us but space and tension.

"What...what's going on?" I ask my gaze going back and forth between Rider, Kane and Lindsay.

"What's going on is my bro here has no game." Kane reaches for Lindsay's hand. She gives me a knowing smile as they disappear into the crowd. "It's a good thing I showed up when I did," Rider says. "My bro sucks at being a good wingman and you could have been on a date with that guy," he says, and points to some random dude at the bar.

I eye him for a second, remembering the game we played when we first met. "Too much hair gel," I say, my heart crashing against my ribs. What exactly is going on here? I'm not sure, have no idea really, but I'll play along for now. "If he leans in for a kiss, he's liable to put my eye out."

"You're right," he says producing his adorable dimple when he grins at me.

"And you might have been set up with her," I say, and gesture to the tall blonde swaying her hips on the dance floor.

"Her legs are far too long." He shakes his head and frowns. "Our kids would have been disproportionate."

"Whew, dodged a bullet there," I say, and wipe my brow.

"And that guy," Rider says, gesturing with a nod as he steps closer his warm scent falling over me. It takes every ounce of strength I have not to throw myself at him. "You would have needed your safe word with him."

"He does kind of look like he keeps his ex in the freezer, doesn't he?"

Rider laughs out loud, and the tension drains from my body. "I've missed you," he says, his voice so low and soft it seeps under my skin and wraps around my shattered heart. My pulse picks up tempo and the room sways as my blood drains to my feet.

"Rider, we can't..." I wave my hand back and forth between our bodies. "...go back to this," I say and take a small step back, his entire presence overwhelming me and making it hard to breathe. "I just...can't." My heart is already broken.

He shakes his head. "Good, I don't want to, either. I don't want to be friends with benefits anymore. In fact, I don't even want to be your friend."

My heart fractures a little more. My God, had he come here tonight just to be cruel to me? I back up even more, and that last glass of wine begins to fog my thoughts. "I...why?"

He doesn't even want to be friends anymore?

He exhales loudly and shakes his head. "I'm an idiot."

"I know."

"Hey," he says feigning offense. "You didn't have to agree that fast." I sniff, and hug myself. "So, Alek—"

I cut him off. "Why the hell is everyone trying to set me up with Alek?" I cry out.

He looks down at his feet for a brief second. "I used to wonder that too."

Okay, none of this is making sense. Maybe his concussion

is making him say crazy things. "I think you should go home, Rider. Go back to bed."

"Kane and Lindsay were behind Alek."

"What? What do you mean behind Alek? And Lindsay never said a word."

"Yeah, I know. Apparently, they thought if I saw you with another guy, it would smarten me up. Smarten you up, too."

I stare at him. Okay, now I really am worried about him. "Rider I think you should sit down."

"Nurses!" he exclaims and throws his hands up.

"Hockey players," I shoot back.

"I don't need to sit down, but we do need to talk." He takes my hands, all humor gone from his face. "When Alek touched you, I saw red. I wanted to kill him."

"What are you saying?"

"I spent my whole life thinking I wasn't good enough. That people only like me because of hockey."

I give a slow nod, and my heart hurts for the little boy no one wanted, a little boy who grew up to be a fun-loving, sensitive, man—who doesn't want me like I want him. "You're wrong, you know," I say quietly.

"I know. I *am* wrong." My head jerks up at that admission. "But after waking up in the hospital bed, and seeing how distant you were suddenly acting—"

"Rider, no," I say quickly to shut him down. "You don't understand. I was terrified. When you went down and blacked out, old hurts and memories bombarded me..." He puts his arms around me, and unable to stop them, tears drench my face. He gently wipes them away. "I was so scared, Rider. You were the first guy I'd opened myself to in a long time. I'd been shut off, afraid to live, love and lose again, but that all changed with you." I put my arms around him, holding him to me, needing to feel his strong heartbeat against my cheek. "... and when you blacked out...scariest moment of my life."

"You love me?"

"Of course I love you. I wanted to tell you that the last time we were together in my bed. But then you talked about setting me up with a teammate." At that realization, I push away. My heart aches in my chest as tears soak my face. "I thought there was more between us. Now you don't even want to be my friend."

"That's because I want to be more, Jules. I want to be your *best* friend, your partner, your husband, the father of your kids." I stand there staring at him, sure I'm hearing things. My knees nearly give and I grip the back of the chair to hold on. "I know this isn't the time or place, but maybe it is since we met here." He pulls something from his pocket. "I was an idiot. I fell in love with you the second I met you. You're fun, funny, sexy as hell, kind, and giving. You spend your life taking care of others, and if you'll let me, I want to spend mine taking care of you the way you need. I used to think hockey was the most important thing in my life, and now I'm not so sure I will ever play again, but one thing I can't do is go in to the future without you by my side."

I hear a small squeal and glance up to see a crowd forming —his teammates and their wives—and Lindsay has her hands to her cheeks, happy tears in her eyes. "Kane and Lindsay were right."

"About what?" I ask, my voice barely a whisper.

"When I saw Alek touch you, it made me face my fears, and I knew you were the one for me and I wanted to be the guy you needed. I'd do anything to be the guy you needed."

My throat tightens to the point of pain. "Rider," I say, and reach for him.

"You were right, too."

"I was?" I choke on my tears, the heavy air in the room almost suffocating. "About what?"

"You told me I needed to go home and go to bed. I do. But I don't want to go there without you. Please say yes and make me the happiest man on the planet." He opens the box and produces the most beautiful ring I've ever seen. No longer able to stand, I sink to my knees.

"Rider, you pushed me away," I say. "You hurt me."

He shakes his head. "We've established that I'm an idiot, right?"

I laugh, and the weight of the world sitting on my shoulders lifts. The air in the room becomes lighter, and I fill my lungs. "Right, we did."

"I want it all, Jules. The good, the bad, the happy and the ugly. I want it all with you," he says, his love and honesty hugging my heart and putting all the pieces back together again.

"Say yes," Alek blurts out and we all laugh. I glance up and realize he brought his teammates—his family—because he wanted to share this with them. He's grown, changed so much since I first met him. So have I.

"Yes," I say. He puts the ring on my finger, picks me up and spins me around until we're both dizzy.

"Dammit, maybe I shouldn't have done that," he says and holds his head.

"You are an idiot," one of his teammates yells, and we laugh again.

"Let's get you home so I can take care of you," I say my heart so full of love for this man that I'm sure I'm going to burst.

"No," he says, his voice so hard and adamant, I freeze for a second. He winks. "Let's get home so I can take care of you, show you I've got game."

"I never doubted that for a minute, Wingman."

Thank You!

Thank you so much for reading The Wingman, book 6 in my Players on Ice series. Please read on for an excerpt of Single Dad Next Door!

Interested in leaving a review? Please do! Reviews help readers connect with books that work for them. I appreciate all reviews, whether positive or negative.

Happy Reading,
  Cathryn

SINGLE DAD NEXT DOOR

Rachel

When my bedroom door flies open and crashes hard against the paint-chipped wall, I groan. "Go away," I say, my voice muffled by my pillow. Not that my roommates will listen, even if they can hear me. Heck, I could scream at the top of my lungs and it wouldn't faze them, much less send them running back to their rooms —not when the view outside my window is that *hot*.

Seriously though, sharing a house with four college freshmen is not my idea of a good time, not when I'm a senior and working my ass off to get into law school. But when I left NYU two months before the start of my fourth year and transferred to Penn State at the last minute, this place was all I could find—and afford. Ultimately, Penn State is where I want to do my law degree after undergrad. I just ended up here sooner, rather than later.

Someone tugs at my pillow and I open one eye to see Becca hovering over me. "Come on, Rach, he just took his shirt off," she says. "You're going to want to see this."

Why oh why did my room have to come with the best view of the hot neighbor's driveway?

"Thank God for this heat wave." Sylvie, roommate number two, fans her face with her hand.

I groan and curl up into the fetal position. I just want one more minute in bed without every member of the house in my room. "I. Don't. Care." Well, that might be a lie. I like looking at the eye candy next door as well as they do, but after putting in a late night at Pizza Villa—I seriously have to find a new job—I need all the sleep I can get before class.

"Jesus, would you look at him," Becca says, her voice a breathy whisper as she peers out the window. "Talk about slurpalicious. I could seriously lick that from head to toe, and back up again."

"Leave," I say on a yawn.

Ignoring me, Sylvie squeals. "He's going back into his garage. Damned if he doesn't look as good going as he does coming."

"But I'd rather see him...*coming*," Becca says, and they start giggling.

"Seriously. Are you both twelve?"

"Shh, he's back," Becca says and swats her hand at me, like I'm an annoying fly that needs to be shooed away.

I shift on my bed, not to get a better look outside my window. No, moving has absolutely nothing at all to do with the shirtless mechanic turning my roommates into dim-witted moths. The *only* reason I'm getting up is to herd these girls from my room, and if I happen to get a glimpse of the hot, tattooed, badass daddy next door, well...then so be it.

I rub the blur from my eyes and toss my pillow at them. "Get away from my window, before he thinks it's me." They don't need to know that the hottie's bedroom window is also across from mine, and that late one night, he caught me staring into his room as he walked around in nothing but boxer shorts. Heck, if they knew that, they'd camp out for the rest of the school year, and that was so not happening.

"Ohmigod!" Sylvie leaps back. "I think he just saw me." She puts her hand over her mouth and starts to giggle. Footsteps pound down the hall, announcing the arrival of my other two roommates. I shake my head as they come bursting in.

Kill. Me. Now.

"Is he out there?" Val asks, her big blue eyes wide and hopeful.

"Yeah, but he saw me looking," Sylvie says. Despite that, she edges back around to sneak another look. Megan hurries across the room, and goes up on her toes to peer over Sylvie's shoulder, trying to catch a glimpse without getting caught.

"Do you really think he killed someone?" Megan asks.

"That's the rumor," Val protests, though her tone holds uncertain convictions.

"Then why isn't he in jail?"

"Maybe it was self-defense."

"He's such a badass."

"He's good with his little girl, though."

"Bad Boy Daddy, now that's hot."

"Do you think he'd spank me if I was bad?"

Unable to put up with their incessant chatter and giggles any longer, I point my finger toward the door. "Out. Now."

A chorus of grumbles ensues as they all sullenly walk to my door. Christ, I'm getting that lock fixed, even if I have to eat ramen noodles for the next month.

"God, you're such a grouch in the morning." Becca shoots me a wounded look over her shoulder.

"Doesn't even have to be the morning," Val adds with a hair toss.

"You need to get your nose out of a book once in a while," Megan says.

"What she needs is to get laid," Sylvie informs them all, but her solution to pretty much everything is sex. Problem is, this time Megan is nodding her head in sad agreement as she follows Sylvie out the door.

"I can hear you," I shout after them. I shake my head and my mussed hair falls over my shoulders. "I'm still right here." As I stand there, dressed only in my tank top and underwear, a warm breeze blows in and slides over my skin, a late reminder that I'd opened my window last night before crawling into bed exhausted. Great. Not only could the hot guy working on his car see my roommates drooling over him, he could *hear* them as well. *And* they just announced that I needed to get laid. How freaking mortifying. I stomp across the room and yell down the hall, "And don't bother to close my door on your way out." As usual my sarcasm is ignored.

I give the door a good slam, which helps improve my mood a little. With a deep breath, I turn around, not to see my hot neighbor, but to close my window. No way do I want him hearing anything else that goes on inside this place, or get the wrong idea that I might want him. I don't. Not in a million years.

I'm completely off guys, trying to keep a low profile. After my ex-boyfriend turned violent and abusive, threatening to kill me if I went to the police, I snuck away under the cover of darkness and put several states between us. He was big and hard like my neighbor, his muscles born from rough carpentry work. Last year, when he came to do repairs on the house I was sharing with friends, I was flattered that I was the object of his attention. At first he was doting and attentive, but as time went by, he became possessive and controlling. I came to find out later, he'd had other charges against him from numerous other women.

Jesus, why am I such a bad judge of character when it comes to men. Oh, probably because my only role model had been a mean-assed, alcoholic father who drove my beautiful, caring mom to an early grave and me out of the house the second I turned eighteen.

If I try hard enough I can still smell the cheap perfume on his shirt when he stumbled in after a weekend-long drinking binge. God, how I hated those women he slept around with almost as much as I hated my Dad. Mom used to try to protect me from his disgusting behavior, but what hurt the most was how he dragged Mom down, aging her pretty face far too early.

My heart squeezes as I think about her. She was a good woman, but was too afraid to leave. Running is hard. I get that now. Not that she really had anywhere to run. Our only other relative was my father's mother. She's still alive, living in upstate Pennsylvania where my Dad was born. While she liked me well enough, when it came to Mom and Dad, she always took Dad's side. That's how it is with parents, I guess.

I lift my arms, place my hands on the frame, and lean in to give it a tug when the hottie slowly lifts his head. Our eyes meet, hold a moment too long, and I suck in a quick breath as heat zings through me—and dammit, it's not the autumn sun that has warmth pooling between my legs.

OMFG.

With a wrench clasped tightly in his right hand he stares at me, like we're in a goddamn Mexican standoff. I swallow hard, and will myself to move, but can't seem to tear my gaze away. Ah, what was that I said about dim-witted moths?

Close the window, Rachel.

While my brain struggles to call the shots, my body has other ideas. Ideas that involve staying exactly where I am and ogling the hottest guy I'd ever seen. Blue eyes, square jaw, a body I could play Plinko on, and low riding, well-worn jeans that accentuate bulges in all the right places, and holy hell, the man has a lot of right places. Want prowls through me, hitting every erogenous spot along the way.

Just shut the window already.

He shifts his stance and taps the wrench against his leg as he looks up at me. A small grin touches his mouth, and that's when I realize I'm half naked. *Please, ground, open up and swallow me.* After hearing the girls, he probably thinks I'm trying to lure him to my room, fix that dry spell I've been going through. I grip the window ledge tighter and slam it down, putting the brakes on my body's reaction, and shutting out six delicious feet of hard muscle and pure testosterone. This is so not what I need right now. Coffee. Yeah, that's what I need. Lots and lots of coffee.

I hurry to the kitchen and shove a pod into the Keurig. I pour milk into a cup and set it on the spill tray. As I wait for the coffee to percolate, I wander into the main level bathroom and glance in the mirror. I look at myself and try to imagine how I appeared through the blue-eyed mechanic's eyes. I see black smudges under tired eyes, boobs that only look big because I'm slender from work, school and lack of proper nutrition and rest. My hair is...wait... I grab a fistful of my curls and examine them closer. Oh, God, pizza sauce.

Could this day get any worse?

Christ, even if he did hear my roommates, I'm sure he'd never look twice at a girl like me—especially the way I look now. A guy like him probably goes out with women who are a little more put together, sexier. Although I have to say in the two months I've lived here, I've never seen a woman come or go from his place. Still, I'm certain a girl next door who always smells like marinara sauce and pepperoni isn't even on his radar.

Good, because I don't want to be.

The coffee machine beeps and I hurry back to the kitchen. I grab the mug to take a big sip. Heavenly. Desperate for a shower, to wash last night's work from my hair, I hurry back upstairs to my room, hot mug of coffee in hand. I check the time and grab my clothes. Giggles come from Sylvie's room across the hall as I dash into the bathroom. I turn the shower to cool, partly because it's just so hot in the house, and partly because I need to calm my overheated body down. I might be off men, especially big, scary ones like my neighbor, but my body and brain aren't working in sync this morning. Clearly my libido didn't get the memo when I left New York.

I stay under the needle-like spray longer than normal, needing an extra minute to clear my head. When the water turns cooler, I jump out, dry off, and pull on a pair of shorts and T-shirt. I towel dry my hair, then tie it back into a ponytail. I forgo makeup. Not only will it melt off my face, I'm not trying to impress anyone or draw any kind of attention to myself. Once done, I grab my purse, shove my textbooks into my backpack, and head for the front door, feeling a little more alive after the coffee.

The hot morning air hits like a slap in the face and I groan. It's October for God's sake. It's supposed to be time for pumpkin spiced lattes. This is more like beach weather. Mother nature needs to get her shit together. I glance at my watch, and judging by the time—thanks to an extra-long shower—I need to get my shit together, too. This morning I'll have to take my car to school, or risk being late for class. The walk to campus is long, around forty-five minutes, but I prefer it on days like today. I need to save my gas money for the colder winter months.

Since my driveway runs parallel to my neighbor's, I keep my head down, toss my backpack into the back seat and climb into the driver's side. Thank God the hottie is out of sight and I don't have to go through the embarrassment of facing him.

I roll my window down and shove the key into the ignition. I turn it, only for the engine to make some god-awful sound and stall out. My heart races quicker. Shit. Shit. Shit. Frustrated, I give the steering wheel a thump with my fist. This can't be happening. I need this car. Need to be able to depend on it if I have to run again. It might be an old junker, but it's all I have. I can't afford a new one. Heck, I'm on such a tight budget, I can't even afford to have this one fixed.

I take a deep breath, throw up a silent prayer, and twist the key again, only for it to cough and gasp, like it's dying a slow and painful death.

No. No. No

A tap comes on the roof, and I turn to see my hot—shirtless—neighbor with his arms braced over the door of my car. He leans down, his beautiful face close to mine. "Need a hand?"

"I...uh...it's not working."

Jeez, way to state the obvious.

He grins, and when I see a cute dimple that contrasts sharply with his chiseled face, I nearly swallow my tongue.

"Yeah, I kind of got that, you know, being a mechanic and all." As he gives off a bad-boy vibe that messes with my common sense, he grabs a cloth from his back pocket, and wipes his hands before leaning into the car, his head practically in my lap.

Holy fuck!

It takes everything, and I mean *everything*, in me not to grab the back of his head and shove it between my legs. My sex practically quivers at the visual. The girls were right. I do need to get laid. I bite the inside of my cheek to stifle the moan rising in my throat.

"What...what are you doing?" I finally manage to ask, and will myself not to writhe restlessly, and show him what a needy girl I really am.

He pulls the hood release, and the front end of my car jumps. His head lifts and once again his face is close to mine.

"Popping the hood." He angles his head, and his eyes narrow. "What did you think I was doing?"

Oh, I don't know. Maybe you were taking this opportunity to go down on me.

"Popping the hood," I say quickly, and try not to think of sex. Dirty sex. Take-me-up-against-the-wall kind of sex. Not that I know anything about that. Sadly.

His laugh is rough and deep as he walks around to the front of the car, and I unbuckle quickly. My legs wobble as I climb out of the driver's seat and follow him. He's grinning when I reach him.

"What?" I ask, my voice raspy.

He touches my cracked windshield washer cap, which I happened to repair all by myself. "Duct tape?" he asks, his voice amused.

"Tools of the trade, right," I say and try not to sound as breathless as I feel. A difficult task considering I'm standing next to a half-naked man that I want to run my hands all over. I mean I've seen shirtless guys before, but come on. This guy is like a freaking viking. He leans forward to fiddle with something, and the movement shows off impressive bicep muscles. I break a sweat as his closeness sends shudders of need between my thighs. Honest to God, the man is a work of art, and all I can think of is no-strings sex—something I've never done before. But that's crazy and reckless and so not me. Truthfully, if I knew what was good for me, I'd slam the hood shut and run in the opposite direction.

I'm about to do just that when he says, "Uh, huh."

"Is...is there something wrong?" Is that my voice? Christ, I sound like I'm whacked out on painkillers.

For God's sake, get it together, girl.

He rubs the scruff on his chin, and I step back, needing a measure of distance before I actually reach out and run my hands over all his hard grooves and deep valleys.

"Plenty," he says again and checks something else. I have no clue what he's doing. I only know that he looks as hot as hell doing it. As he leans over my car, my gaze slides to his ass, committing the way his pants cup his cheeks to memory. The guy could be in a jeans commercial, or better yet, a Calvin Klein underwear ad. I'm a girl, but advertising like that would have me one-clicking the buy button.

My heart hammers as he stands again. He turns toward me, but I'm far too slow to react. His eyes are piercing, almost a deeper shade of blue when my gaze jerks to his, and I can't tell whether he's thrilled or pissed to find me checking him out.

I step closer and look over the engine. "So, what is it?" I ask, disgusted with myself. I should not be fantasizing over this man.

He clears his throat. "I think the first thing we need to do is replace the spark plugs," he answers, his voice a little hoarse.

"Yeah, that's what I was thinking," I say, my head bobbing in agreement.

That grin is back when I look at him. "You know something about cars?"

I shrug. "Sure...and duck tape."

He laughs and says, "It's not..." he shakes his head. "Never mind. So, you agree then, that something's not firing right?"

Firing? Oh, things were firing all right, and lighting up my body like a goddamn Fourth of July celebration.

Damn him.

Damn Mother Nature.

Damn dim-witted moths.

ABOUT CATHRYN

New York Times and *USA today* Bestselling author, Cathryn is a wife, mom, sister, daughter, and friend. She loves dogs, sunny weather, anything chocolate (she never says no to a brownie) pizza and red wine. She has two teenagers who keep her busy with their never ending activities, and a husband who is convinced he can turn her into a mixed martial arts fan. Cathryn can never find balance in her life, is always trying to find time to go to the gym, can never keep up with emails, Facebook or Twitter and tries to write page-turning books that her readers will love.

Connect with Cathryn:
Newsletter
https://app.mailerlite.com/webforms/landing/c1f8n1
Twitter: https://twitter.com/writercatfox
Facebook:
https://www.facebook.com/AuthorCathrynFox?ref=hl
Blog: http://cathrynfox.com/blog/
Goodreads:
https://www.goodreads.com/author/show/91799.Cathryn_Fox

Pinterest http://www.pinterest.com/catkalen/

Hands On

Hands On

Body Contact

Full Exposure

Dossier

Private Reserve

House Rules

Under Pressure

Big Catch

Brazilian Fantasy

Improper Proposal

Boys of Beachville

Good at Being Bad

Igniting the Bad Boy

Bad Girl Therapy

Stone Cliff Series:

Crashing Down

Wasted Summer

Love Lessons

Wrapped Up

Eternal Pleasure Series

Instinctive

Impulsive

Indulgent

Sun Stroked Series

Seaside Seduction

Deep Desire

Private Pleasure

Captured and Claimed Series:

Yours to Take

Yours to Teach

Yours to Keep

Firefighter Heat Series

Fever

Siren

Flash Fire

Playing For Keeps Series

Slow Ride

Wild Ride

Sweet Ride

Breaking the Rules:

Hold Me Down Hard

Pin Me Up Proper

Tie Me Down Tight

Stand Alone Title:

Hands on with the CEO

Torn Between Two Brothers

Holiday Spirit

Unleashed

Knocking on Demon's Door

Web of Desire